WHITE POINTER

JOHN LEE SCHNEIDER

D0916139

SEVERED PRESS
HOBART TASMANIA

WHITE POINTER

Copyright © 2018 John Lee Schneider

WWW.SEVEREDPRESS.COM

ISBN: 978-1-925840-34-6

'Can't you feel them circling, honey? Can't you feel them schoolin' around? You got fins to the left, fins to the right, And you're the only bait in town'

Jimmy Buffet

CHAPTER 1

The bites were fresh... and they had bled.

Carson frowned. That meant they had occurred before death. Very likely they occurred at the TIME of death.

The choppy surf rocked her little boat, bumping the hull roughly into the whale carcass she had found floating just beyond the breakers, roughly six miles south from Surf Shore.

Pulling her little outboard up alongside, wrestling with the ocean, she hooked a gaff into the floating meat, pulling close for a better look. Once stable, she pulled out her tape measure and spread it across one of the largest bites.

The whale was a small one – a baleen calf – not yet half-grown. Still, it reached well past both ends of her little fourteen-footer, and she was conscious of its dead weight as it rocked in the current. It certainly weighed more than she and her tiny boat did together – a boat that was getting on in years, and perhaps a bit rickety.

Truth to tell, she really shouldn't have it out this far – it was really just a rec boat she'd had ever since her brief stint in college – a ski-boat.

Of course, even back then, she often took it out well-past the breakers. She'd been flagged by the Coast Guard once, after venturing into the shipping lanes. She'd been nineteen at the time, with a boat-full of drunk sorority sisters, who she'd managed to talk into a late-night joyride that had somehow gotten off course.

Carson had been called a daredevil more than once. In point of fact, it had actually been a sticking point that had helped end her last relationship – and as her own father had said at the time, 'considering her ex, that's saying something'.

Her father had deliberately used the non-pejorative descriptive noun, 'ex', as Carson had forbidden his actual name be spoken aloud.

Still, it was a remark that had not been helpful in the immediate wake of what was a fairly reluctant – and painful - separation.

For one thing, Carson resented the characterization. She was not 'reckless' – not in her world, at least.

A better description – also coming from her not-to-be-named ex – was 'fearless'.

And, of course, she freely admitted that there was nothing that pissed her off more than being told to 'take it easy' – except maybe for being told 'no'.

Or even worse – sputter, snarl – that she was 'wrong'.

Case in point, was why she continued to motor about in her taped-up little ski-boat – and her own position on the subject was inarguable.

She liked to feel the ocean – for which, she had an undeniable knack, for sure. The little boat allowed her to skip across the surface like a well-tossed stone – a surfer with a long-honed acuity to the rhythms of the sea.

On the other hand, however, if for the odd moment, she happened to leave the wheel unattended – like, say, if she was leaning precariously over the side in rough water – she recognized how the smallish boat could be a definite liability.

As if on cue, a sneaky wave bumped her hull up against the whale's carcass and, for one hairy instant, she slipped towards the water, before catching hold of the gaff she had latched into the floating blubber, and pulled herself steady to its side.

The maneuver finally gave her a moment of sufficient stability to read 'twenty-eight inches' across the tape measure, stretched out across the bite – the one that had bled. The big one.

It had hit the little whale just below what would have been the hip on a human – taking out the target's tail.

It took a big shark to do that. A damn big shark.

Big enough to take a whale – a small whale, to be sure, but a whale nonetheless.

That was something that, as far as Carson knew, had not been seen in modern oceans – dating back to the days of Megalodon.

There had once been whale killers in the ocean – and they had hit just like this – taking out the tail, and then simply retreating, waiting for the subject to die, feeding at their leisure.

Modern white sharks preferred much smaller prey – mostly seals and sea lions. Very rarely, Carson had seen a target as big as a walrus.

In fact, locally, hits on seals had been way up this year. Carson had spent the last few weeks following a trail right along this particular coastline, where 'Seal Rescue' teams had reported carcasses bitten and killed, but then not eaten, suggesting not only a lot of sharks, but a lot of seals – enough to trigger the attack reflexes even when the big whites weren't hungry.

But a whale was something different. Carson had never heard of it before.

Of course, there were always white shark bites all over whale carcasses – as there was all over this one. But these whales had most likely died of natural causes, or were the victims of whalers or orcas. The white sharks simply dog-piled on the left-over corpse. Sailors, back in the day, called them 'dogfish'.

Modern shark predation on whales was strictly relegated to 'scavenging'.

But not this time.

The bite radius indicated an attacking animal of six meters or better. And it had gone after an animal even bigger than itself.

Well, Carson thought, she was out here looking for the unusual, and this certainly qualified.

She pulled out her phone and tapped the screen awake.

CHAPTER 2

Carson knew 'shark attack' was right near the bottom of major causes of human death – you were more likely to die of a lightning strike or a dog bite than a shark attack.

Still, it *did* happen. It had happened right here in the waters off Surf Shore – and it had happened more than once – repeatedly, actually, like clockwork over the course of the last several years.

Out of no less than seven attacks on humans, five surfers, two kayakers, four had been fatal.

And they had been dramatically fatal. When a white shark hits a target for real – with real predatory intent, as opposed to the curious little bite-and-spit 'attacks' – victims are usually killed on point of impact. The victims that survived were the ones where the shark had actually made contact with their kayak, or their surfboard. But they were all predatory, 'Polaris' style strikes.

They had also all occurred during the same time of year – two on nearly the same date, two years apart.

This had led to uneasy speculation about a single shark being responsible.

And while Carson knew better than to believe in the 'man-eating rogue shark' – the JAWS monster that specifically targets humans – she recognized that it *was* possible that a particularly aggressive shark might hit the same beaches as part of a regular migration route.

Carson – whose entire life had been dedicated to the preservation of wildlife – especially large, spectacular wildlife – was uncomfortably aware of a number of potential suspects – suspects she literally knew by name.

The last thing she wanted was to see them hunted down.

She sighed, glancing over the side – the rolling carcass in the water, however, could not be ignored.

A dead whale was significant. This was something new.

The bites along the side indicated a very large shark, but not preternaturally so – since the fishing bans, nineteen and twenty feet was not outside the range of adult females – there were at least half-a-dozen individuals Carson had personally documented in the area that could have fit the bill.

There were always a lot of big sharks out there. But this was more significant than just size.

What these bites represented was a behavior shift.

As Great Whites matured, their targeted prey changed – as small bodied juveniles, cold-blooded fish were sufficient. But after a certain size, they needed more protein to fuel the engine – hence the fat-layered diet of pinnipeds.

Perhaps after a certain size, their calorie requirements spiked again?

Wasn't that, after all, the evolutionary path that had once led to Megalodon?

Carson tapped her phone again, dialing a number.

After a moment, her phone identified 'Lauren' – an incoming text.

It read: "Underwater. What'cha got?"

Carson smiled. She knew Lauren was working her last few days on an expiring grant and was taking every last opportunity to get out on the water. Right now, she was likely halfway up the north coast, probably with a crew of interns, and certainly somewhere near the Farallons – a particular hot spot for white shark activity, where Lauren liked to focus most of her research.

They had entered college together, and Lauren had stayed the academic route. But Carson had quickly jettisoned the trappings of academia – despite the strenuous objections from her father – and she simply launched her life into the sea.

And while Carson knew Lauren valued the credentials and authority that came with academics, she also knew her friend envied her freedom.

There was another beep on her phone – question mark with an explanation point.

Lauren also liked to text underwater – she had sent Carson several selfies from shark cages, with big whites circling in the background.

Carson had returned one of herself, hanging off a Great White's dorsal fin in a free swim.

And boy, *that* had started a fight with her ex when she got home.

Her phone beeped again, and Carson tapped a brief message.

"You won't *believe* what I've found."

She snapped several shots of the whale carcass, showing the tape measure spread across the huge bites, and then hit 'send'.

After a fairly long pause, Lauren responded: "Think it was the shark that took it out?"

Carson: "Yep."

"Think it was local?"

"Looks fresh."

There was a longer pause. Then another text beeped in: "Seen any other sharks? It's dead around here."

Carson frowned. That was significant as well. The Farallons were usually high-traffic at this time of year.

She typed back. "There's more than one bite on this whale."

The message came back from Lauren: "Be careful."

Carson shook her head and typed, "Okay, MOM."

Without waiting for a response, she switched her phone off.

It figures, she thought, now that Cody was gone...

Damn – said his name – 'EX'! EX, EX, EX!

Carson sighed.

Now that 'Cody' was gone, Lauren naturally had to step in as a surrogate – to 'look after her'.

Carson had known Lauren a long time – people often thought they were sisters. But Lauren was always 'big sister'.

It was ironic, Carson supposed – what she always professed to drive her nuts about her ex (okay, fine...'Cody'), was exactly what she turned to in her BFF.

Psychology. Go figure.

Then you could throw in the abiding fact that, even though she had dated Cody for almost a year and a half, Lauren had never met him.

Lauren had believed that to be on-purpose for Carson's part.

And she would have been perfectly right. Cody and Lauren would not have gotten along.

Cody was something of an anomaly among the surf crowd – not to look at, really – no, there he was the very definition of a surf-beach rat – but certainly in attitude. In particular, his love for the ocean did not translate to romantic illusion.

The insinuation, of course, when he said it out-loud, was that, in HER case, it did.

After one of the attacks last season, several surfers who had witnessed the incident – this one a hit on a kayak, where the target had survived – had been interviewed on the beach. In between the 'dudes' and 'whoa, mans', they had pretty much parroted the old saw about 'gotta live with the ecology.' Dude.

Cody hadn't much patience with that sort of 'fuzzy-headed Earther-crap' – a phrase that Carson found particularly irritating and noticed he pulled out whenever he felt like picking a fight.

Blanket statements were another.

The reason, Cody had explained, as if she were a four-year-old child, behind the increasing shark attacks in California, was a no-brainer – it was the fishing ban – pure and simple. Combined with a ban on hunting seals – the white sharks' primary food... as large adults – and BOTH populations exploded.

"Conservationists," Cody had told her, smiling ironically, in that maddeningly self-assured way of his, "are *always* pulling this kind of crap."

Carson had not answered, refusing to be baited.

"They did the same thing in Australia," Cody continued, mildly. "Now they're killing people. Ask any abalone diver what he thinks of the fishing ban."

Carson let herself be dragged in.

"That's not fair. You're talking about people who are willingly putting themselves in a prey environment."

Cody's eyebrow raised. "Like surfers?"

Carson frowned, her brow furrowed in a slow simmer.

Cody shrugged. "Seems to me, there wasn't a problem until conservationists decided to load-up a predator/prey environment right next to a high-population human habitat. And then sell it as a recreational area."

Carson had nearly hit him then. Instead, she had simply stood up and slammed the door on her way out, leaving Cody to spend the better part of the next two days apologizing.

During those two days, Carson never consciously acknowledged that last barbed comment, focusing instead on her temper – which Cody had really gotten going on that particular occasion... perhaps for the near-treasonous reason that he might have a point.

For one, she knew he was perfectly right about the hunting bans. Populations that – thirty years ago – had been in trouble, were now booming.

Unfortunately, traditional patterns had already been disrupted – the effect of attempting to *not* have an effect, instead created the opposite effect – ecological congestion.

And it had been a bountiful year – survivability had been good.

There were a *lot* of sharks this year. They were big and fat.

And a big shark had been hitting the area for several seasons now.

That was a problem for conservationists. If you campaign for an animal that turns around and kills someone, that made it harder.

It wasn't the shark's fault, of course, but it was remarkably unhelpful for their own PR.

And while you couldn't let people be killed, Carson knew perfectly well, how such incidents got blown out of proportion.

The possibility of a single shark being involved in some or all of the attacks also raised concerns that, until recently, she hadn't even considered.

For example, recent breakthroughs in DNA testing might actually allow a 'fingerprint' to identify an attacking animal. Tooth fragments from victims had been salvaged, and collecting tissue samples from several of the big sharks in the area might actually enable them to pinpoint a specific individual – something that, even a few years ago, Carson would have dismissed as a near-impossibility.

And while Carson also knew the possibility of a single attacking animal was not as far-fetched as some seemed to believe – white sharks were very habitual, and the attack incidents *did* seem to match the two-year migrant patterns of the big females – to say so would reintroduce a variation of the 'rogue-shark' myth back into the public psyche – a negative misconception that had taken decades to discredit.

OR, as Cody had pointed out, it might draw attention – and perhaps criticism – to the practical effect of conserving apex predators.

"See," he had told her, his face indulgent and patient, with not the slightest hint of sarcasm, "your odds of getting struck by lightning go way up if you stand on a hillside in a storm, holding a metal pole.

"Like you said," he continued, using another time-proven tactic of turning her words back at her, "put yourself in a prey environment and it's not a long-shot anymore, is it? More of a probability, really. And now you've got one right off a popular surf beach."

"So what do you want to do?" Carson had returned sharply. "Just go out and kill them all again? You can't blame the sharks! It's not their fault!"

Cody had shrugged. "I get it. They're just being sharks. It's all very natural behavior. All I'm doing is asking you to recognize that it IS their natural behavior."

Now he had turned to her, eyeing her in that particularly infuriating way he did when he was certain he was about to make a telling point... because he 'understood' her.

She got ready to be pissed.

"Say you *did* find that one shark was behind it all. And say you were able to identify it. What would you do then? Would you fish it out? Just that one?"

He had waited a moment, watching for a reaction.

The question, however, had pushed her momentarily back on her heels.

"Well?" Cody had asked again. "What are your priorities?"

Thinking back on it now, Carson believed that had been the beginning of the end for the two of them.

She deeply resented the suggestion that she would put the life of a fish before a person, let alone allow anyone to be killed.

But she did not readily have an answer to his question.

Carson personally knew the sharks here.

She and Lauren had been cataloging them for years, tagging them, recording them by fins and markings. And lots of cage diving – *any* excuse to cage-dive.

They posted online footage of themselves – a pair of blond California beauties, in bikinis, swimming with sharks – their videos went viral.

The sharks were characters. They had even given them names – as well as personalities to go with them.

One of their favorites, for example, was a big, particularly dominant female, who had been returning to the coast for years – a powerful, five-thousand-pound beast they called 'Big Rhonda'.

Rhonda was always the first to signal her presence each season with those dramatic, breaching attacks that carried her two-ton body fifteen feet clear of the water.

There were others. Besides Big Rhonda, there was a smaller, but temperamental male they called 'Mack the Knife'. He was an even more regular visitor, especially through the Farallons – following the annual migration patterns of males. Mack was known for his particularly acrobatic strikes on the fat elephant seals that populated that patch of rocks – Lauren had even given him the sub-nickname, 'Mack the Mako' for his hang-time above the water.

Then there was the older, stealthier, 'Bloody Mary' – another big female – instantly recognizable for the ugly scarring that marked her hide – likely mating scars (or 'love bites' as Carson called them).

Bloody Mary was so named because she always seemed to appear from behind you – just like the lady in the mirror. She was less showy than Big Rhonda, but Carson had often wondered whether it was because she was less dominant, or perhaps just experienced enough to let Rhonda do all the heavy lifting. Mary was almost always the first among the free-loaders to show up whenever Rhonda hit a big seal.

This particular shark was also never baited into attacking decoys – but known to hit two of three seals a season. And she never missed.

They were all unique, magnificent animals. And Carson was willing to admit to herself that any one of them could be responsible for any of the attacks off Surf Shore.

She was further willing to admit – at least privately to herself – that, no, she would not happily see any one of them fished out.

Tag it. Put a tracker on it. Something.

But she couldn't say that to Cody – not after that crack about priorities – not with that mild expression on his face just waiting to turn knowing and cynical.

It had been shortly after that – almost exactly two years ago, now – when Carson had done her free-swim – the one she had texted to Lauren. The video had shown her swimming in the open ocean with Bloody Mary, hanging onto her dorsal fin, Mary cruising serenely, as if oblivious to the strange little lamprey clinging to her fin.

It was always about moods, Carson explained later – picking your moments. She had let Mary circle her cage, letting her test and bump the metal, discarding the notion that the strange object in the water was food, before getting out in open water with her.

Carson had been part of a charter that day. Her cage-mate was a grad student who had volunteered to shoot video for their next on-line production. To his credit, the somewhat nervous-looking young man had stayed steady and filmed the entire episode, after Carson had gotten out, grabbing hold of Mary's fin as she passed.

Besides timing, there was positioning. Seals often circled white sharks in open water – hanging back, just behind their dorsals – out of biting range – and the sharks never bothered them. For one thing, seals were highly maneuverable, and millions of years of evolution had bred into the shark the knowledge that she couldn't reach them from there.

Where you didn't want a big white was *behind* you.

Where it knew you couldn't see them coming.

As long as Mary knew Carson could see her, and held her position, she was safe.

Although, Carson considered, she wasn't quite sure she would have pulled the same stunt with Rhonda.

The video, of course, went viral.

Cody, of course, had blown a gasket.

In fact, that had been the fight that had really ended it. They had not quite been living together – Carson kept her own place – her own space – but it had been Cody that had walked out that night – his own apartment, in fact – and he had not come home. Carson had left in the morning, and while Cody did finally call – more than once, in fact – that was the last time she had ever stayed over.

During one of those last conversations before she'd officially ended it, he had tried once more to apologize – spoken in a voice that didn't believe for a second he was in the wrong, but still wasn't ready to lose her.

Of course, the resignation in his voice suggested he already knew he would.

He might have been a cowboy, but she was a mustang. Too wild to be tamed.

"Utterly fearless," Cody had told her in those last days. "And damnedably foolish."

Then his phone had clicked off in her ear.

If only it had just ended then. But it had grown typically, acrimoniously worse. By the time it was over, it was *really* over.

Sitting alone on the boat, momentarily lost in her thoughts, Carson suddenly smacked the railing, smarting her hand.

Frustrated that she still missed him.

And sitting alone on the boat, Carson suddenly felt very alone, very isolated – something she never felt when she was on the ocean – usually, it was a sensory rush – far from lonely, if anything, it was an almost communal sensation of being part of *everything* – a comfort to the spirit.

But just now, it was instead a feeling of being very small.

There was a light thump from below.

Carson stood, looking over the side, seeing nothing.

On the breeze, however, an odd sound carried on the wind.

She frowned. It almost sounded like... car traffic. Honking. Or maybe the call of sea-gulls – perhaps attracted by the whale carcass.

Except she could see no gulls. She held her hands to block the sun, looking back at the rocky coast.

She paused for a moment, hanging on the sound.

Then, in a spark of realization, she picked up her binoculars, turning towards shore, and focused in on the narrow stretch of beach that divided the expanse of sheer rock.

"Well, I'll be damned," she said aloud.

Because suddenly she understood... everything. About the attacks, the presence of the sharks – everything.

She pulled out her phone and began to type.

A message to Lauren: "You *really* won't believe this."

She was interrupted, however, by another hit from below – this one a pretty good jolt.

Startled, Carson was rocked in her seat, nearly dropping her phone. For a moment, she thought the waves had slammed her into the whale carcass.

Then she saw the circling dorsal fin, angling lazily away from the side of the boat.

The saw-shaped notches identified her right away – Big Rhonda.

She had likely been lurking below all along.

Then Carson looked down at the sudden rush of water at her feet.

Leaning over the side, she could see a large hole bitten in the side of her little boat. Water was bubbling through.

Carson blinked at the hole for several seconds before the full import struck her.

Her first reaction was, ironically enough, anger – anger at Cody.

Because this was just the sort of thing he always warned her about.

She could even hear him bringing up the abalone divers – gold hunters, she had called them – who had willingly put themselves in a prey environment.

Carson almost laughed at herself. She was already arguing back in her head – no stubbornness in her family.

Of course, she wasn't like an abalone diver – she wasn't out here for personal gain. She was a researcher – a conservationist.

Who deliberately put herself in a prey environment.

See? It WAS different.

The water at her feet was now soaking her shoes.

She was sinking.

Carson turned her head towards the rocky coast.

How far out? A mile?

She started the motor, which turned over quickly, but even as she did so, the small boat listed badly.

The water was nearly up to the railing.

Beyond the railing, hovering not quite out of sight, was another fin, that had joined Big Rhonda in a slow, lazy lap around the floating whale corpse.

Likely, there were half-a-dozen more circling below. Bloody Mary, maybe Mack the Knife. Maybe even a few newbies.

It had been a bountiful year.

They were big and fat.

The first of the water began to seep over the railing.

"Oh my God," Carson breathed.

She glanced at the life-jacket Cody had always insisted she kept on board.

As if.

A moment later, the motor sputtered and quit.

CHAPTER 3

Lauren loved the Farallons.

Perhaps it was an odd thing to say, but there was something quietly spectacular about this lonely stretch of rocks. It was such an untamed stretch of ocean – too jagged to attract boats, barren and inhospitable, yet barely twenty-five miles off the coast of one of the most populated modern cities in the world.

Something about that appealed to Lauren – the idea that such a pure, primordial ecosystem continued to exist with impunity, just beyond the borders of civilization.

Seals milled on the beach this time of year.

And below the rough surface, just beyond the rocks, was where you found the sharks.

An older world existed here – an avenue to a time before humankind.

Just now, however, it was desolate and empty. She had spent the last hour in a cage, looking mostly at gray-blue water and nothing else.

The 'men in gray suits' as they had been nicknamed by surfers in Australia – a gangster's pinstripe image – had been a no show.

This season, Lauren had joined a small research crew, and was provided with a boat just big enough to carry a cage and a winch, manned by a three-person crew of two grad-students – Bob and John, both scuba-aficionados – and one unpaid intern – an aspiring marine biologist named Suzy.

It wasn't Cousteau, but it sure beat Carson's rickety little outboard.

That was one of the perks of academia – she sometimes got to play with equipment like this. The bad news was, it ended tomorrow.

And today – the last several weeks, in fact – there had been nothing.

It was starting to be early afternoon; Lauren and her small crew were calling it a day.

No one spoke. Bob and John broke down the collapsible cage. Suzy started up the boat, turning it out of the small cluster of rocks where they had anchored, and began to turn in the direction of shore.

Lauren sat by herself, up on the top deck, looking out at the inexplicably empty water.

This season, the Farallons were a lonely place.

There were a lot of urban legends about this stretch of water, especially circling around the surfer-crowd. Local gangsters were rumored to dispose of bodies out here – fed to the sharks – sometimes alive. It was further rumored that these incidents were often filmed – possibly for purposes of intimidation – perhaps just for souvenirs.

It had also been suggested, in whispered tones, that the practice had made the local sharks hungry for human flesh.

Lauren found that last part frustrating. It just goes to show – human murderers feeding people to fish, and somehow the fish gets the blame.

She often told anyone willing to listen – certainly she'd repeated herself often enough to her captive audience aboard the boat – that most of the rumors were simply just that. First of all, it wasn't even quite fair to call any shark 'local' – they migrated across oceans.

Second, it had been demonstrated, time and time again, that whites didn't like eating humans. Even people hit by evidently predatory attacks were rarely eaten – human body frames hardly carried the calories worth the biological effort to digest. Great Whites were nothing if not a marvel of energy conservation. If whatever they bit didn't taste like the big protein ball of a seal they were expecting, they most often spat it out.

Most often.

As for the other legends... well, Lauren did happen to know of a certain video that had wound up in police hands. She herself had been brought in for an expert's analysis.

It was a pirated montage of attack footage – on human beings. A Great White 'snuff' film. And it did look as if it had been filmed in the Farallons.

Lauren's own verdict had been 'inconclusive'. With modern CGI techniques, she couldn't be sure.

She could not, however, point to anything in particular to discredit it.

She also adhered to the rule, if one person can think of it, another person can do it. Lauren doubted it had not been done.

Although, even if had, that did not make sharks 'man-eaters'. All they did was follow their instincts. When attacks did happen, it was because something had pushed that instinctual trigger. It was just that simple.

On the other hand, Lauren allowed that predators do learn, and will adapt different techniques – adapting to change – perhaps a new food source. Perhaps a new stress form, such as an increase in population – congestion.

And the result, of course, was more attack incidents. It simply stood to reason.

But even that was blown out of proportion. It was still only a few incidents, separated by years - hardly the danger of driving a car.

And Lauren was ashamed to admit she herself had exploited the incidents – it was why she was out here today. The attacks off Surf Shore, in particular, were the leverage she had used to extend her grant through this season.

Truth to tell, she had been so shameless she had actually used her own attack incident to sell it.

It wasn't really even an attack – she had been in a cage.

But it had been here in the Farallons – nearly this same spot, almost two years ago.

It was, in fact, the very incident that Lauren had texted off to Carson.

From Lauren's end, it had actually been pretty hairy. One particularly large and aggressive male had hit the cage in a full-on vertical attack. It was a fairly unusual occurrence – in fact, it was really the only incident she could think of where the shark seemed to have deliberately attacked a cage, especially after inspecting it over several passes.

Likely, it was a territorial impulse – something large in the water, in a high-population, high-prey environment.

It gave them quite a jolt. It was a fifteen-foot, twenty-five-hundred-pound animal, and it had actually left a dent in the bars. This was what Lauren had been showing Carson in her selfie, even as the aggressive male continued to circle just behind.

Carson, of course, had apparently taken it as a dare, and proceeded to one-up her with a free-swim, hanging off the fin of a notoriously large and, in Lauren's opinion, particularly sneaky and dangerous female – one that probably had two-thousand pounds on the shark that had hit her own cage.

As Lauren heard it later, that free-swim had started quite a fight at home – even as it was going viral online – and as it happened, it also turned out to be instrumental in the eventual break-up over the following weeks.

And while Lauren remained critical of Carson's little stunt, she couldn't complain about that.

Lauren had never met Mr. Cody Martin, but she knew the word going around. Standard beach fair, of the sort that prowled the waves, like sharks themselves, for the Valley Girls that recreated on Surf Shore.

Carson had always kept her relationships sequestered – something Lauren never quite understood... although, from what she heard, there was good reason with Cody. While Carson might not have brought him around, she did talk about him an awful damn lot – always with his most pejorative comments fresh on her tongue.

For nearly two years, Carson was either with the guy, or bitching about him, and Lauren had actually begun to hate him herself. Especially, after some of her own comments got traded back at her.

Carson actually seemed to encourage the second-hand friction. For Lauren, it was like a sparring match of barbs with an opponent she had never even met – like a chess game played by mail. She had quietly cheered when Carson had, at long last, called to report their final separation.

On the other hand, since they had split, Carson had been... different.

Guys had come and gone before – Carson was never shy of attention – and Lauren had never seen her give any of them more than a casual 'Que sera sera,' as she sent them on their way. In fact, after she'd first met Cody, Carson had actually flat dumped a guy – a well-to-do pre-med student (who Lauren ALSO had never met, but was apparently from a good family and Carson's mother had liked very much) – who she'd been seeing for the previous six months.

This same med student had appeared back on the scene shortly after Carson had split with Cody. And while Lauren didn't know all the details, pre-med had ended up with a broken nose, and Cody had spent a night in jail.

Carson had, of course, inspired fisticuffs before – more than one beach brawl had erupted over her attentions. And in Lauren's humble opinion, Carson enjoyed it immensely.

Some people just lived on adrenaline – the rush of life was like wind in their faces.

And Lauren supposed it was Cody who had said it best – she was utterly fearless.

It had been Carson who had first taken her out on the open ocean – much to the retroactive disapproval of Lauren's own father, who quickly learned to pay attention whenever the two of them, who everyone thought were sisters – maybe twins – ever embarked out the door together.

By the time they were in their early teens, they were staples among the beach-set, and by the time they reached college – or at least Lauren did – they were semi-famous, locally – particularly Carson, who in addition to surfing competitions, wasn't above the odd bikini, or wet-t-shirt contest.

That was another example of the particular courage Carson possessed. In fact, Lauren often worried for her friend, even as she found herself following along on each ensuing story-waiting-to-happen, which could have been anything from a wild night on the town, to skydiving – and this was long before anyone had even suggested diving with sharks.

It had, in fact, been Lauren (and Lauren's sorority sisters), sitting next to Carson when the Coast Guard had discovered their little boat well out past the breakers, sometime after midnight. As her own father had chastised her at the time, it might have been Carson's idea, "but you were right there with her, weren't you?"

It was, of course, also Carson's idea to start the video series. Swimming with sharks. Lauren's father hadn't even been able to rationally comment on that one.

In bikinis, of course. Carson even had a professionally-made mermaid's tail – apparently a gift from one of the movie studios – a donation to her website – and she would actually free-dive as deep as sixty-feet or better, gliding among dolphins, reef sharks – even creatures as big as manta rays, and once, a feeding, forty-foot whale shark.

Their passion together, however, was Great Whites.

Lauren herself couldn't quite articulate why.

Perhaps it was simply the attraction of that older world – a quasi-mystical place, where sea-monsters were real – monsters, magic, and dragons. Like the fantasy novels she had lived in as a kid.

In a way, it was odd that she herself would end up on the science side of it – she, who fancied herself the dreamer of the two, pursued her button-down and rational degree – perhaps a by-product of living in the library as a young girl – while Carson, who in her own odd way, was the hard-core realist – lived like a nymph on the ocean.

Of course, now that she was a grad student, Lauren was back on the water. Field research, of course. That was why she was out here at the Farallons – part of a white shark cataloging project that had been going on for nearly six years. And here in the Farallons, was where to reliably find them this time of year.

Except, Lauren thought, frowning, this year they simply weren't here.

It had been a remarkably dead season – and by all accounts, this should have matched up with the two-year migration cycle of several big females on their books, so there should be mating as well as hunting going on.

But she had not seen a single shark all season.

The seals were here – there was no reason the sharks shouldn't be.

Lauren uncomfortably remembered the old saw that it was 'too quiet' – right before hell broke loose.

But after next week, her money ran out. Today was her last day with the boat – an expensive loaner from a local charter captain, that came with the expiring grant – leaving a funding gap that had yet to be filled. She was looking at deskwork back at the institute until a new donor came along – which meant the foreseeable future.

The sharks' absence, however, was actually more of a mystery than might be readily apparent – primarily because Lauren knew they had to be out there somewhere. And for sure she knew they were down south – Carson's text-message had confirmed that much. But why not here in the Farallons? This was where the big females congregated, loading up calories – it was at the end of a dry stretch along the coast, where the pickings were slim, and the sharks took full advantage.

But they weren't here this year. Lauren had put out decoys behind her boat, chummed the water, and nothing.

There was only one time that she remembered when the Farallons had seen such a mass departure of the big whites.

Carson remembered the incident from when she was just a kid – it had been widely reported at the time.

An orca – a killer whale – had attacked and killed a Great White Shark in full view of a boat-full of researchers, who had filmed the incident for posterity.

At the time, much had been made of how the shark – otherwise the alpha-predator in the ocean – had been so easily taken down. The whale had hit it from below, stunning the shark, and then simply flipped it over on its back, inducing tonic immobility, and then had towed the hapless fish until it drowned – whereupon, the orca, in typical cheeky fashion, had paraded its catch in front of its human audience on the boat.

The incident was quickly famous worldwide. But it was the aftermath that was perhaps even more remarkable, and it was something that wasn't immediately apparent.

It was reported later that, after the attack, the rest of the sharks had vanished. There wasn't one seen for the entire rest of the season.

That had led to speculation among scientists, not only of why, but of how.

Clearly the orcas were the catalyst – the obviously dominant predator, and the sharks were willing to cede the entire seal season to them. But as to how this actually happened was open to question.

Some suggested that the dead shark-meat released a chemical into the surrounding water – sharks had been shown to be spurned by the smell of their own dead – there had been some success with chemical shark-repellents based along this line – or it could have been the sonar blips of the orcas themselves, picked up by the sharks' own sensitive senses, who simply heard them and left the territory – with one unfortunate straggler.

And while Lauren had not seen any orcas in the Farallons this year, they *had* been reported in high-numbers, all up along the coast. Could their very presence be driving the sharks out of such a lucrative feeding spot as the Farallons?

If so, that led to another relevant question, and that was, where did the sharks go?

At least some of them, it seemed, had shown up off Surf Shore.

Lauren glanced back down at the message Carson had sent her. A whale – apparently killed by a predatory attack from a white shark.

As she did so, she realized she had two new messages – they would have come just as her team was pulling her cage up over the side – she hadn't heard the beep.

She clicked the first one. Then the second.

At the second message, Lauren blinked, as if she wasn't sure she was reading it right.

Then her eyes widened as the import struck her.

She tapped Carson's number and hit 'dial', putting the phone to her ear.

The line rang. After a moment it rang again. Then a third time.

On the tenth ring, Lauren hung up and dialed the Coast Guard's emergency line.

CHAPTER 4

Carson's funeral was three days later.

Mounted on a stand, surrounded by flowers, was a poster-sized portrait. No casket.

No need for one.

On the wall above, playing on a full-size screen, was a video show of Carson's life.

Standing at the back of the little chapel, where she had volunteered as hostess for guests signing the log-book, Lauren felt like she was looking back at her life too.

Only now that life was put in a different perspective.

As always, Carson dazzled onscreen, dancing undersea with dolphins and whales – the giant manta ray. They had left in the scene with the big whale shark – it really looked more like a big catfish, after all.

They had, however, tactfully edited out bits where she had been swimming with sharks.

In a way, Lauren thought, it was a shame – it had been such a focal point of her life, and to separate her from it, was leaving out so much of who she was.

On the other hand...she got why.

But for Lauren herself, there was more than enough on screen right now to bring home how close it had always been.

In a kaleidoscope of broken light, Carson twirled like a ballerina next to the six-ton whale shark – a mild-mannered plankton eater – as it fed upon the krill at the surface.

This was one where she was wearing the mermaid's tail – and as she moved underwater, she was graceful beyond all description – a free-dive of more than forty-feet.

Yet even as the audience members – her family and friends – murmured appropriately, Lauren found herself frowning just a little bit.

Carson had pulled it off well, but the footage on-screen had been taken at extremely high-risk. She was down deep, and the mermaid outfit was cumbersome, hampering her maneuverability.

Then there had been the moment where the shark's massive tail – fully ten-feet tall – had stroked directly into her path. Carson had dodged it, fading back into a spin, as she slipped aside, letting the passage of water carry her as the crushing blow missed her by barely two feet.

But she had pulled it. And she had made it look easy. Her family watching posthumously actually rippled a bit of laughter at the moment – all unaware of what they had just seen.

Carson had never even mentioned the moment at all – perhaps didn't even remember it – no more than any surfer plans a wave. She just casually pulled it, and she did it every day of her life, as effortless as a mountain goat living on a rocky ledge.

You just got to trust it, after a while, Lauren thought – that ability to pull long odds.

And then one day, you realize you've just been lucky all along.

Carson hadn't died swimming with the whale shark that day simply because the tail had missed her.

Perhaps, when all was said and done, as the grief process set in, the most blindsiding, gut-kicking part of it all was that – despite all of her own big-sister worrying – Lauren had started to believe in Carson's magic – that whatever happened, she would pull it.

The tail would miss her.

Then one day it hadn't.

Nothing of her had even been found.

Truth to tell, based on what was likely to be left behind, Lauren hoped nothing ever was.

And while she was sure Carson, if she could have chosen, might well have preferred to die in the ocean... not like this.

Lauren had been on site with the Coast Guard that day – it was the last day with her boat, but the institute let her take it down the coast to Surf Shore – she was the expert, after all – and she had arrived on the scene to find several police patrol boats had joined the Coast Guard. Carson had likely called them herself.

The guard commander was a long-term veteran named Shaw – Lieutenant Quinton Shaw, a SEAL officer, who had retired to the Guard – long enough on the job to know Carson and Lauren by name. Lieutenant Shaw had, in point of fact, been the very one that had accosted them on their drunken college stunt out past the breakers that night.

Now his face was grim as he recognized Lauren waving at him.

They had found the smashed remains of Carson's glorified little dingy, a high school jalopy, that had dared the choppy waters of the Pacific almost every day of its useful life.

The bite in the hull told its own story.

As the police boats circled, corralling the wreckage, Lauren thought back to how many times they had been out on that little boat together – one year, for a joke, Lauren had bought her a JAWS t-shirt with the caption, "You're gonna need a bigger boat."

All it took was one bite.

Once the boat was salvaged, Lauren provided whatever minimal elaboration that she could.

The wreckage had likely been pulled by the tide several miles from where the incident occurred – there was no sign of any floating whale carcass – and in Lauren's opinion, based on Carson's itinerary, the actual attack happened somewhere beyond the south point of Surf Shore.

And it was definitely a white shark. She estimated its size, based on the bite marks, at around six meters.

Lieutenant Shaw had spread his arm over the hole in the little boat's hull.

"How many get this big?" he asked.

Lauren shook her head. "Not many."

Although, Lauren thought, there WAS at least one or two that she could think of, right off hand.

For a moment, she had looked at the final text Carson had sent her. She debated, for a moment, putting it on the record.

In the end, she had not. There was not much more they needed to know anyway.

Lauren had asked to be the one to call Carson's parents. It had been her father that answered.

Carson's father – who Lauren still called 'Mr. Sheridan' – and who was just like Lauren – despite it all, he always believed whatever magic that had carried his daughter this far would take her the rest of the way. Lauren could literally hear that magic die in his voice as she told him.

Amazingly, he had asked Lauren if she was okay. He had thanked her, and then hung up to go tell his wife.

Mr. and Mrs. Sheridan were at the front row, now, as the small compilation film began to reach its end. The little chapel was crowded – the Sheridans had initially wanted a private service, but Carson just had too many friends to turn away – the little chapel was full to capacity, with plastic chairs lined beyond the pews into the hall. And as the little life story flickered to a stop, there was a moment before the lights came back on, where the congregation sat silent in the dark

The door opened in that moment, drawing attention from the sunlight glaring in.

The figure at the door paused, staring into the darkness, as if confused.

Then the lights came on, and Lauren recognized the face of Cody Martin – a face until that moment, she'd only seen in jpegs.

There was a murmur in the hall as the attendance recognized his face. Lauren saw a frown on Carson's father.

Cody blinked at the entire congregation staring back at him, and for a moment, it seemed as if he might simply step back out and leave.

Then he glanced over at Lauren, standing there with the guest book – giving her a momentary double-take, but apparently with no idea who she was – and, without a word, he had signed in, stepping discretely to stand quietly along the back wall as the main service began.

CHAPTER 5

After a moment, the murmur in the congregation quieted, and the elderly priest-for-hire began to give the church eulogy. After he was done, a number of family and friends took the stage, including Lauren herself, to speak their final words about Carson Sheridan.

But even as she waited for her turn at the podium, Lauren found her eyes turning towards the lone figure huddled by himself at the back of the chapel, looking down to the floor, ignoring the darkened expressions of Carson's parents, as well as a certain well-to-do pre-med student, whom Carson's mother had liked so much.

She thought about what she knew about Cody Martin.

It gave you an idea how compartmentalized Carson had always kept her life, that this was the first time she'd actually seen him in person. Lauren always wondered why she was like that.

Perhaps it was as simple as not bringing her man around other women. Carson was oddly primal in that way.

Oddly feral – perhaps it was that touch of wildness that attuned her so well with nature.

And now, as Lauren looked back at him, she figured that was why Carson had gone for Cody in the first place.

He hadn't looked like much in pictures – scruffy – an unkempt surf-bum. And he didn't look like much more here.

On the other hand, like most beach rats who lived on the surf and the water, his rumpled dress hung over a wave-carved musculature – just the sort of guy Carson had always favored on nights when she had a little too much to drink – those nights when the feral overcame the rational. And even Lauren would admit that a guy like Cody was a perfectly acceptable animal.

They hadn't met in a nightclub, however, where Lauren could have run blocker. They had met on that all-powerful plane of mutual interest – Cody was teaching a scuba class.

When combined with simple mutual physical lust, actually having compatible, as well as passionate interests, was perhaps the single biggest attractor beyond the structure of the atom.

Lauren had seen it in her when it had happened. Carson had never fallen in 'love' – not that Lauren ever knew – not really. There were infatuations, crushes – a couple of flings – always with Lauren herself as the true significant other.

Then all of a sudden, there was THIS guy.

Lauren had wondered at the time if she was jealous. She had comforted herself that, jealous or not, Carson could do a lot better than some surf-bum.

Of course, the 'better deal' that had swooped in after their break-up – likely due to an invite from Carson's mother – was currently sitting two aisles over from where Lauren currently stood.

'Pre-med' – Carson hadn't even talked about that guy enough for Lauren to remember his name. But he sat front row, with the family, and was periodically scowling to the point of distraction over his shoulder at Cody standing in back – brows furrowed over a nose that was somewhat more crooked than it used to be.

Lauren took her turn on stage, and as she did so, she saw Cody's eyes turn up, looking at her oddly – not with recognition, so much as someone who was seeing a ghost.

She knew she and Carson looked alike. Maybe that was it.

Lauren looked down at the few notes she had prepared and began to speak.

She was the last on stage. When she was done, the chapel priest said a few more words, and then the video began to play again.

Carson's father took the stage and thanked everyone for coming.

Then it was over. The congregation rose from their seats and began to filter towards the doors.

At the back, Cody quickly stepped before the crowd, and exited the same way he had come.

Out of the corner of her eye, Lauren saw pre-med start to move after him, only to be quickly collared by Carson's father, who clapped him patiently on the back, shaking his head reproachfully, until Cody was out of sight and gone.

Lauren frowned, looking after him.

She pulled out her phone, clicking through a series of pictures. She found one of Carson and Cody, back in better times, out on a boat, decked out in scuba gear.

She looked up in the direction Cody had disappeared. After a moment, she stepped into the milling crowd after him.

CHAPTER 6

Cody was half-way down the block before Lauren made it through the crowd out on to the street. She saw him already standing at the corner, waiting for the light, and moved quickly to follow.

As she did so, she saw a short, balding man, in wire-rim glasses and a goatee, approach, sidling up like a stray cat poking around a garbage can. Cody stiffened up as the man stepped up beside him.

Lauren couldn't hear the exchange, but saw Cody turn slowly, with an obvious air of menace, and for a moment, she thought he might actually up and slug the guy.

Instead, she saw him poke the guy in the chest and, as his voiced raised, the words carried.

"I know exactly who you are. You're the one who ran my mugshot on the front page. So how 'bout you pound sand, you little prick."

Lauren could hear the man's easy, unconcerned response, tapping the poking finger. "That's assault you just committed there, Mr. Martin."

The cross signal changed. Cody stood glowering an extra moment, before turning, stalking across the intersection.

Lauren stepped up to a trot behind him, glancing curiously at the bald man – who seemed to be suppressing a smirk – as she passed.

Cody was on the far side, moving quickly, with a touch of temper in his step.

He had arrived at a small, beat-up pick-up, of indeterminate color, and was digging in his pocket for his keys, when Lauren caught up with him. A frown darkened his face as her hand fell on his shoulder.

"Excuse me?" Lauren said, removing her hand.

With a resigned sigh, Cody turned.

"Yes," he said, carefully neutral. "Can I help you, Miss?"

Lauren held up her phone, showing the image she had pulled up. "This is you, right? I mean... you're Cody?"

He looked at the picture for a moment, his face expressionless. But he nodded.

"That's me," he said, and when he looked back up, his eyes had softened somewhat.

"You're Lauren. I've heard of you."

Lauren nodded. "I've heard of you too."

"For a second, I thought you might be her sister."

"People say we look alike."

Cody's lip twitched, as if with an attempt at an ironic smile. "They say that do they? Well, they're right."

There was an awkward silence as they regarded each other – two people, aware of each other for years, meeting for the first time.

"So," Cody said finally, "Lauren. Can I help you with something?"

Lauren shrugged. "I wanted to meet you."

Cody blinked. "Why?"

He shook his head and now he half-chuckled. But there was no humor in it.

"I'm sorry," he said. "Look...Lauren... I know exactly who you are."

He stepped forward abruptly, and while his voice remained mild, he looked her right in the eye as he spoke.

"You're Carson's 'angry best friend'. Oh yeah, I've heard of you. For almost two years, I heard all about you. Usually when she was telling me something that crucified my character, all my motivations, and generally cast me as a scumbag – it usually sourced back to you."

Lauren blinked, taken momentarily aback. Then her own temper sparked a bit.

"Excuse me," she replied, hands moving to her hips, 'but aren't you the one who referred to me as the 'Super-Bitch from Hell'?"

Now he smiled a little, this one a little more genuine.

"Yeah," he said, "that sounds like one of mine."

Cody glanced back across the street, towards the church, where a number of people were now looking over. Carson's parents, and her pre-med, would-be ex, were among them.

The smile quickly faded, and the stoic separation returned.

"Listen," he said, "I'm sorry, alright? I guess my defenses are up."

Across the street, pre-med was postured in a steady glare. Cody shook his head tiredly.

"I almost didn't show," he said, and now his shoulders slumped. "I know absolutely no one here today wants me around."

His eyes turned away from the chapel, his gaze drifting off to the west, in the direction of the beach, where less than a mile away, you could hear the subdued roar of the surf.

"The thing is," he said, "I don't really care about anybody here."

His voice had grown soft, as if he were now talking to himself.

"I had to be here," he said.

And then with the smallest crack: "I had to be."

He fell silent, his eyes still searching for the ocean, as if for comfort, just out of sight over the few blocks of buildings. His stoic face remained resolute.

Then he blinked, waking, glancing unhappily off towards the church and the grouping of Carson's friends and family, before turning briefly back to Lauren with the cynical half-smile again touching his lips.

"And now," he said, "I guess I can go, and not darken anyone's life around here, ever again."

The half-smile flashed in Lauren's direction, severing contact.

"It was nice meeting you Lauren," he said, his voice that close to polite – it didn't QUITE sound like 'go to hell'. Probably, he was being respectful of the occasion.

He turned back to his beater pick-up, his hand again rifling through his pocket for his keys as he slid into the driver's seat, apparently ready to make good on his word.

Lauren stood silent for a moment, ready to let him go.

Then she glanced down at her phone, at the picture she had pulled – Carson and Cody out on his boat – a bigger boat, she remembered Carson saying – another point of contention – Cody had refused to even climb on board her 'little death-trap'.

Ironic, Lauren thought, considering the piecemeal carny-wreck of a pickup she saw before her now. The boat in the picture was solid and well-maintained.

Surfer's priorities, Lauren thought. That was probably where he spent his money, while he let his land-lubber rig go to pot.

Cody cranked the pickup's sputtering engine alive, and was shifting the struggling transmission into gear when, on impulse, Lauren tapped his window.

Frowning, Cody rolled the glass down, looking up at her with waning patience.

"Listen," she said, "can we go somewhere and talk?"

Cody's nettled expression never changed. But after a long, indecisive pause, he leaned over and unlocked the passenger door.

"Okay," he said. "Get in."

CHAPTER 7

"Who was that guy trying to talk to you back there?"

The two of them were sitting at a little café, just a few blocks away – a vegetarian house Lauren and Carson had once frequented. It had one of those menus with a calorie count, as well as detailing the organic-grown ingredients, and how good it all was for the environment.

Cody, had arched an eyebrow as he read the menu, but said nothing.

"I'm buying," Lauren said.

Cody smiled thinly. "Really, thank you. I'm not hungry." He shrugged, closing the menu. "Or a rabbit."

Lauren's lips pursed.

Carson had said he knew how to push buttons. Up until today, Lauren had only experienced it second-hand. She closed her own menu.

"Why were you yelling at that guy on the street?"

Cody looked up, sharply. "I wasn't 'yelling,' for crying out loud. Jesus."

Lauren saw his hand involuntarily clench, bumping the table in just a tap of frustration. And for the first time, his defensive expression suddenly looked more embarrassed and ashamed.

"Alright, fine," he said. "That guy works for one of the local dailies. Carson's dad has a little money, and he's friends with the editor. That guy..." Cody tossed a thumb over his shoulder as if he were standing behind him, "... is the guy that put my mugshot on page one, after I got arrested. I made the six o'clock news, too."

Lauren's head cocked. "But you *did* it, right? I mean, you punched a guy's lights out. It's not like they made that part up."

Cody looked back at her, resigned.

"What do you want from me?" He shook his head. "You know the story, don't you? I punched Carson's pre-med frat-boy. It wasn't entirely self-defense."

Cody leaned back in his seat, arms folded.

"You wanna hear me say it? I hit him because I wanted to. I knew he was a better catch – money, security – the whole future thing – gonna be a doctor, for Christ's sake."

Cody shrugged.

"I was jealous and angry because she left me for a better deal, so I punched the guy. And I spent the night in jail for it. AND the guy wanted to press charges, so I *could* have gone to jail for a lot longer than that. Still could, if I get out of line."

"That," he said, "was why I didn't pop that little bastard out on the street today.

"It's also," he continued, "why Carson's family thinks I'm a dirtbag."

Cody considered.

"No," he said, "scratch that. They always thought I was a dirtbag."

There was a heartbeat of silence as, for the first time, Cody's eyes dropped.

"I guess that was just when I sort of started to agree with them."

His voice had taken that low tone again, as if he were talking to himself.

"When I got out the next day, that's when I decided to just leave her alone."

When he looked back up, his lips were crooked in that half-cynical hint of a smile.

"Best thing I could do for her, right?"

Lauren personally remembered that little stretch of time – she had gone through it all over on Carson's side of the fence – *all* the drama – the tears, the nights of over-indulgent booze – and of course, pre-med, when he first started skulking back around – particularly when he had showed up one day with a busted nose.

Carson had sent her a jpeg – two-black eyes swelled-up behind a taped-on bandage – with the text below: "Cody stopped by today."

As if she wasn't ridiculously, vainly pleased by the whole incident.

Lauren herself had appealed to her friend's reason by invoking simple biology – actually a variation of what she had been trying to tell her all along – from the moment Cody had appeared on the scene.

Carson's attraction was natural enough – it was a psychological reaction to physical/chemical stimuli. Lauren had made an effort to pound this point home early on. There was a purpose for guys like Cody, she explained – Cody was for fun – a good rap and good rhythm between the sheets – a 'one-nighter', she had said, not to put too fine a point on it – *not* someone you call back in the morning.

Across the table, Cody nodded knowingly, as if reading her thoughts.

"After all," Cody said, again eyeing Lauren directly, "wouldn't it be stupid to throw her future away over what amounted to a chemically-induced euphoric high?"

Lauren blinked at her thoughts spoken back to her.

Cody was nodding. "Yeah, Carson told me that one too."

Lauren cleared her voice. "I simply advised her with the cool head that she didn't have. Like a friend does."

She shrugged. "You two had chemistry," she said. "But that's just hormones and hang-ups."

Cody nodded indulgently.

"Yes, you have identified key ingredients in the recipe," he said. "You *do* get the significance of 'more than the sum of its parts', don't you?"

He leaned back in his chair again, squeaking the floor this time.

"Funny thing is," he said, "I'll bet you don't even believe your own bullshit."

His eyes narrowed.

"Yeah. I know your type. I can see it in your eyes. All cynic – but pining all the while."

He nodded slowly, with a chirp of humorless laughter. "Didn't stop you from throwing salt on MY tail, though, did it?"

His voice rose with this last, and a couple of the other patrons glanced over. Cody frowned, huddling back down again, that same brief flash of shame across his face.

When he looked up again, his eyes were serious.

"Why are we talking, Lauren?"

Lauren stared back, indecisive for a moment. Was she certain she wanted to take this route?

Cody came from the feral part of Carson's life. How close did she really want to associate?

As she studied his face, however, what she saw was a similar, fresh grief, that was mirrored in her own eyes, but combined with a pile of regret and frustration... yet still making a fair effort to be civil.

'Fair effort', if not entirely successful. But that was enough to decide her.

"I got a text from her," she said. "Right before...before."

Lauren brought up the message: 'You *really* won't believe this!"

She looked up seriously. "She found something out there."

Cody was shaking his head. "What? What do you mean?"

"Well...," Lauren tapped a few pictures up. "She sent me these."

She flipped through several shots of the dead whale carcass, with the huge bites taken out of it.

Cody frowned at the images.

"A dead whale. Sharks eating it. What about it?"

"She said she thought the shark took it out."

Cody absorbed this silently.

"But the last message came later," Lauren said. "She found something else."

"What? What are you getting at?" Cody was shaking his head. "Why are you telling me all this?"

"Because she was out there looking for reasons for all the shark activity in the area."

"I've said it a hundred times," Cody said tiredly. "It's over-population."

"Maybe so," Lauren countered. "But why does it keep happening here, specifically?"

"They're creatures of habit." Cody shrugged. "What's the point?"

"The point is," Lauren said, "that I want to go back out there. I want to try and find what she did."

Cody frowned. "You might find more than you want," he said. "So what's stopping you?"

"I don't have a boat." Now Lauren popped up the image of Cody and Carson on her phone again. She tapped the screen for emphasis. "You do."

Cody stared back at her incredulously. "Are you kidding me? That's what this is about? You're trying to schmooze me up for my boat?"

Lauren felt a static spark of temper but patted it down.

"Don't you want to know what happened to her?"

Cody pushed away from the table.

"I know what happened to her," he said. "What happened to her was what I always was afraid would happen to her. It really is, literally, my worst fuckin' nightmare."

At that, Cody stood.

"And frankly," he continued, "I don't want to think about it anymore."

He tossed a couple bucks on the table. "Give it to the waitress – for the water."

Then he turned to leave.

Sitting there, Lauren finally lost the battle with her temper.

"You really are a bum," she said, her voice low and venomous. "She deserved a hell of a lot better than you."

She said it loudly, and people were looking in their direction again.

Cody was still standing, half-turned, staring down. For a moment, the intensity in his eyes actually seemed a little scary – Lauren reminded herself that this guy had been in jail for assault, after all.

But then he sat back down, glancing uncomfortably over his shoulder as the other customers were now openly watching them.

Lauren lowered her voice.

"Carson found a couple of things out there," she said. "One of them was a whale that had been killed by a shark. You live on the ocean. When have you *ever* heard of anything like that?"

Cody shook his head noncommittally.

"But whatever she found next," Lauren continued, "*That* was something I *really* wouldn't believe. Those were her words. Doesn't that raise even a little curiosity in you?"

Cody stared back silently.

Lauren allowed herself a bark of cynical laughter.

"I mean, seriously – what the hell else are you going to be doing, anyway?"

Her phone sat on the table between them, with Carson's image smiling back at them, face up. Cody reached out gingerly, tapping the image, and it disappeared.

Then abruptly, he stood back up again.

"All right," he said simply. "Let's go."

CHAPTER 8

It was still early afternoon when they reached the small stretch of rocky coast that lay like a craggy obstacle course, just south of Surf Shore.

Shielding her eyes from the glare, Lauren pointed out past the point, where the sandy beach ended, and the coastline simply broke off into sheer cliffs, mining the surf beyond with layers of jagged reefs.

Less than two-hundred yards off-shore, the ocean dropped off abruptly into deep canyons – perfect for ambush attacks from below.

"This is where she was headed," Lauren said, squinting towards the coastline. Cody was holding a respectful distance from the sharp rocks, but now he began to veer back towards shore.

"Right here," Lauren said again. "The... wreckage was found about six miles up the coast."

She considered. "You know," she said, thinking out loud, "another day or two and I'd have probably been out here with her." She pointed north. "I was up in the Farallons that day. This is seal season. But the sharks weren't there."

Cody glanced up. "I've seen orcas this year."

Lauren nodded, taking quiet note that Cody recognized the ecological significance of that.

"Great Whites will cede territory to Killer Whales," she said. "That would explain them missing from the Farallons. But why come here? I mean why here specifically?"

Cody said nothing, angling his boat through the chop.

The swells were large – all the more intimidating for the wall of bladed rock that replaced the public beaches that lay just a few miles north.

Cody cursed under his breath as he navigated the rough surf, shaking his head. "I can't believe she'd take that little piecer outboard of hers out in this shit."

Lauren said nothing, but the irony was not lost on her, as she clung to the little boat's railing as it fought through the waves.

While it looked like it might once have been a commercial fishing boat – solid rigging, with a winch mounted on back for pulling in nets – the general size and design was evocative of the SS Minnow.

On a moment's reflection, Lauren thought it was revealing that he would chide Carson for her little outboard while captaining a boat that was only marginally larger. In fact, it might even be indicative of a core point of the friction that had finally come between them.

It all boiled down to acceptable risk. Cody was a personality that took it to the line... but not over.

He also demonstrated an impatience for carelessness like that of a firefighter – someone who lived a life of carefully regulated risk – where oversteps could make a real difference.

On short acquaintance, Lauren realized his role, in regards to Carson, was rather similar to her own – an anchor.

Lauren wondered if it was the sort of thing Carson sought out deliberately – perhaps a defense mechanism against her own wild nature – making sure she had a spotter in shouting distance.

It was also not a coincidence that the separation from Cody came when that anchor had made a bid for the pilot's seat.

Lauren could see that in him too – especially if he'd decided her safety was his personal responsibility.

Although, truth to tell, she completely understood.

"She used to scare me too, you know," Lauren said.

Cody glanced back without comment.

"Seriously," Lauren said. "That video with the whale shark – I shot that. She was hovering in sixty-feet of water in a free dive. So, yeah, she used to scare the hell out of me."

Lauren shook her head.

"She always pulled it, though. I used to call her 'Calypso'. She was just one with the sea."

Cody didn't look back. "Yeah, so's any bait-fish."

The remark hung on the air, heavier than it had perhaps been intended – weighed down by the brutal truth of it.

Perhaps realizing it, it was Cody who broke the moment of uncomfortable silence.

"You're right, though," he said. "She could get you believing in it."

He shook his head. "But I always knew better."

Cody eased back on the throttle as they approached the first of the jagged procession of rocks that guarded this section of the coast. Lauren noticed the same ease of movement she had always seen in Carson herself, as Cody drifted them casually past the craggy reefs.

There was less chop as they grew closer to shore, but the swells were larger.

As they crested, Lauren spotted something in the water just ahead.

"Hold on," Lauren said suddenly, standing up and pointing. "What's that?"

After a moment, the rolling waves revealed a white, bulbous mass floating just beyond the rocks.

"Well, well," Cody said, as they pulled up beside it. "What have we got here?"

Lulling with the tide, pushing ever closer to shore, was the whale carcass Carson had stumbled upon three days before.

Lauren estimated nearly two-thirds of the mass of the thing had disappeared since the snapshots seen just a few days ago. For an animal that was mostly blubber, the whale calf was nearly skeletonized. It looked like a pack of piranha had been at it.

Cody reached a gaff into the remaining blubber, pulling them alongside the floating carcass.

"That's a lot of sharks to do that," he said.

Lauren pulled out her own phone, snapping a few shots for comparison.

A lot of sharks, alright.

A lot of BIG sharks.

She looked around at the surrounding water – apparently empty – but she knew they were there.

They had been trolling the coast at a safe distance from the rocks, but that still left a good half-a-mile to a sheer cliff – maybe another mile north or south to reach a spot where you could actually climb out.

What would it be like to go down around here? What would that moment be like when you realized you had to swim for it?

Looking around at the seemingly dead-still water – so different from the abandoned Farallons – Lauren felt an unaccustomed tremor of fear.

Something around here had hit a whale – and then had hit a boat.

They were now in a bigger boat. But not a *lot* bigger boat.

She glanced over at Cody – who she had judged on short acquaintance, as someone who pushed the edge – but certain of his limits.

Perhaps the disquiet Lauren saw in his eyes had something to do with the parameters of those limits suddenly not being so certain.

"Heard a story out of Australia," Cody said, as he shielded his eyes from the sun, pointing off towards the unwelcoming rocks. "These guys got swamped about a mile off shore – an abalone diving team – they got hit by a rogue wave that turned them over."

Cody tossed a dismissive hand wave out over the energetic water that currently bounced them up against the diminished whale carcass.

"This is nothing," he said. "Sneaker waves out there will flat flip you over. And it left these two guys hanging on an upside-down hull."

Lauren said nothing – she had heard something about this incident – others like it as well.

"The diver swam to shore," Cody continued. "The skipper stayed behind." Cody glanced meaningfully up at Lauren – again showing that uncanny ability to mirror her thoughts. "Some guys," he said, "if you put them out a mile or so and tell them to swim for it, they freeze up – they won't do it."

Cody shrugged. "Well, they never found the guy that stayed behind. They found the boat. That, and a torn-up life-jacket."

Lauren shut her eyes, hoping Cody wouldn't continue – ready to say something if he did – but he fell silent.

It didn't matter – the image had been set.

What would that swim back have been like?

Or what about that moment, clinging to the boat, when you realized there was something poking around from below?

As if on cue, there was a light tap from beneath their feet.

Cody glanced up, brows raised.

Lauren was gripping the stern, eyes wide as she looked around at the surrounding ocean.

The whale carcass rocked against them, with a heavy thump. Had that been it?

But Cody was shaking his head, as if with the same thought.

"Nope," he said, "that came from below."

There was a fixed compartment behind the main cabin, and Cody popped it open.

Inside – among other things – were what looked like several tall cans of beer – the type with pull tabs. Cody grabbed one up, taking it to the side, pulling the tab and dropping it into the water.

The foul stench reached Lauren's nose – an aerosol blast of rotting foulness – and her stomach retched rebelliously.

"Oh, Jesus," she gagged. "What the hell is that?"

"Chemical repellent," Cody said, looking over the side as the releasing pressure, twisted and spun the canister below the surface, clouding the water.

"Stinks, doesn't it? It's made out of dead white shark guts."

Lauren was still battling with her stomach. She frowned at the thought of the rancid chemicals being released into the environment, although she again recalled the famous white shark-exodus from the Farallons after the orca attack in '98 – an incident that many had attributed to the release of just such chemicals. Lauren had heard of some success with repellents based along similar lines. In fact, river-dwelling bull sharks, had also responded to predator pheromones, extracted from crocodiles, but almost all species tested had reacted strongest when presented with scent from their own kind.

Sharks didn't seem to like the smell of their own dead.

And for the moment, it seemed to have worked. Long minutes passed, and whatever had hit their boat had not come back. The water remained empty. The sharks – if any had truly been skulking about – had gone.

Cody glanced up, approvingly. "That's a repellent that really seems to work," he said. "At least within a confined area."

He tapped a CD player mounted just inside the cabin window, laboriously attached to what looked like an old, sixties-style sound system – complete with a microphone hanging out onto the deck.

"I also play orca sounds," he explained, smiling. "I don't know if that one works or not, but I'm willing to try anything."

He shrugged, eyeing her meaningfully. "Don't always gotta fish 'em out, if you can drive 'em off. Right?"

Lauren said nothing – not sure if the remark was face-value, or patronizing. Still, it was a fair statement, either way.

And truth to tell, she felt a little relieved that whatever nasty concoction he'd dumped into the water, chemical or no chemical, seemed to have worked.

Although, Lauren thought uneasily, glancing at the still-meaty whale carcass, any prowling sharks likely would not linger far.

Perhaps this was a good time to leave this particular prey environment. Lauren was feeling uneasy in a way she couldn't remember having felt out on the ocean, at any time before.

Possibly, it was just a stress reaction to Carson's death.

On the other hand, it was also fair to say they were seeing things she hadn't seen before.

It was also possible the jitters in her spine were those instinctive danger-signals, that only sentient humans, alone among all animals, ever seemed to ignore.

Cody seemed to feel it as well. He pushed away from the floating whale and steered the boat back towards open water – still slow to evade rocks, but working back the way they had come.

"You know," he said, glancing back at her, "this place is giving me the creeps. It just *feels* dangerous."

Lauren glanced back as the floating whale drifted into the distance.

"Yeah," she said, in a small voice, "it does."

"Something's wrong, out here," he said.

Lauren said nothing.

There was. He was right. You could feel it.

They were moving out of the shallows now. Cody frowned, glancing back over his shoulder, his brows furrowed as if in thought.

Abruptly, he turned south again, picking up speed as he circled further around the next point – a spot where the cliff jettied out and the rocks were particularly jagged – a brief, inhospitable peninsula interrupting the otherwise solid wall of cliff.

Lauren glanced nervously back to where they'd left the floating whale. "Wait a minute! Where are we going?"

She held on as Cody picked up speed, cresting the peak of the abbreviated peninsula, before suddenly stopping altogether and turning off the engine.

The ocean was rougher out this far. Lauren's heart did a quick little flip flop as she latched onto the railing.

"WHAT are we doing?"

"Quiet, a minute," Cody said, suddenly standing, head cocked. "Listen."

For a moment, there was nothing but the waves.

Then, distant over the rush of water and wind, came a burbling warble – like the sound of congested traffic – out of place and out of context.

"Do you hear that?" Cody slapped the railing. "Do you?"

Lauren frowned. "What is it?"

Cody was nodding as he started the boat back up.

"Oh, I think I know."

He cranked the engine, and now he was slaloming between the big swells until the little boat dropped into the little cusp of a cove beyond the point.

It wasn't an obvious refuge – surrounded by rock – certainly not attractive for boats. But it was a nice little cul-de-sac, that broke both the wind and the surf. The crash-bang of the open ocean dropped off almost immediately to low comfortable swells. In farmer's terms they sat in the 'lee of the stone', between two rocky peaks.

And in the little auditorium, the sounds that carried on the wind, echoed off the canyon walls – barks, honks, squeals.

Between the rocks was a short, but substantial rocky beach – perhaps a hundred yards, all told – as well as a water-worn crest into the rock, creating a sort of stair-step directly above.

Lined along both shelves, protected from the worst of the elements, were mobs of elephant seals.

An entire new colony, and no one had a clue it was there – just a few miles down from the beaches.

Cody turned a raised eyebrow in Lauren's direction.

"I think we've solved our mystery," he said.

Lauren pulled out her phone, taking video of the crowd of swarming pinnipeds.

It wasn't a big colony – probably just a migratory rest-stop. But it was well-protected – a spot where they were not likely to be bothered by humans, with the open ocean only meters away.

And because they were there, so were the sharks, waiting beyond the reefs, where the land-shelf dropped off into the deeper depths – just at the edge of sight.

CHAPTER 9

"It didn't have to happen. A hundred times over, it didn't have to happen."

Cody leaned on the throttle as he steered them back into deeper waters, heading back up the coast for home. The engine revved – a touch unnecessarily – like squealing tires in a burst of temper.

"I mean, my God!" Cody said, rapping his fist along his dash hard enough to leave a dent. "This is it," he said, shaking his head, frustrated. "This is exactly what we were fighting about all along."

Lauren stayed discreetly silent, clinging to her seat.

Cody glanced at her briefly, as if irritated by her silence.

"So," he said, "you found out what you wanted to know. What's your next move?"

A direct question – he wasn't about to let her just sit there and not engage.

"I guess I'll have to talk to some people at the institute first."

With a pinch of visible blood pressure, Cody touched the throttle just a little more.

"What about the Coast Guard? Or the cops?"

"Yes. They will have to be informed."

"Not the press?"

"What good would that do?"

"It would warn people."

"We'll warn people," Lauren said, a touch crossly. "We'll inform the authorities of the situation here, but let's get some experts to talk it over before we just go shouting to the press. We don't want to start a panic."

The throttle ticked up another notch. Lauren glanced at Cody nervously.

He wasn't looking at her now, but his posture had taken that of a cat with its hackles up.

"What you mean," Cody said, his voice deliberately calm, and perhaps a bit more intimidating because of it, "is that you want a minute to spin it so you can avoid a bunch of bad press for Great Whites."

He was picking a fight, Lauren thought, archly – and he was pretty good at it too. That was something else Carson had said. He'd pick it, and keep at it until you were in it with him.

"That's not fair," she said patiently. "We'll warn people, but we'll do it responsibly. And no, I don't want people suddenly hating sharks. Of course, I don't want that. After JAWS came out, Great Whites were almost hunted to extinction. That hurts the whole ecosystem."

"Yeah," Cody returned quickly, "forty years ago. But now you conservationists have thrown nature just as far out of whack as the over-fishing. You don't think doubling the population is just as invasive?"

"So what do YOU want to do?" Lauren said, feeling her temper start to helplessly slip. "Just go and kill them all again?"

Cody turned on her now, with the impatience of a long-worn sore spot.

"There," he said. "Right there. That's your problem. I didn't say that, did I? I didn't say, 'hunt to extinction'."

Shaking his head, he turned back to the wheel, and now he was really peeling out, knocking Lauren back in her chair.

"That's how it is with all you eco-types," Cody said angrily. "It's not your ideals – it's your methods. And the control-freak personalities that go with them. You're all absolutists. All extremists. I say we start fishing them again, all with reasonable limits, or seasons – and maybe even taking out a problem animal or two. But you call it extermination."

He shook his head. "You people just don't get it. You're like a doctor that never stops medicating. You're an army of friggin' marching brooms."

Now he cranked the boat hard east, and began heading towards shore, the sudden lurch again nearly knocking Lauren from her seat.

"I mean, here you are, prattling about the ecology. Easy to say until you're on a surfboard with a two-ton predator coming at you at thirty miles an hour, face-first, with a mouthful of teeth."

He was almost shouting now, competing with the engine.

"I mean, for crying out loud, use a lick of sense! 'Over-population' means they aren't 'endangered' anymore. You can stop protecting alligators once they start showing up in people's bathtubs. Stop protecting crocodiles when they start grabbing children from streams running through suburban backyards. And you can, for Christ's sake, stop protecting man-eating sharks when they start killing people."

Lauren knew he was venting – holding forth – and more importantly, grieving – but the show of temper was still beginning to frighten her. They were coming up on the docks now, at seemingly breakneck speed, and Cody seemed not to be paying attention.

Besides, he wasn't the only one grieving.

"Carson didn't think so," she said, perhaps a bit more sharply than she intended, but the combination of grief and anger threatened tears – which made her even angrier.

"You can't blame the sharks for being what they are." Lauren was shouting back now.

"I don't," Cody shouted right back. "I blame thirty years of eco-nuts who put the welfare of fish – of man-eating sharks – above the lives of people."

Lauren smacked the console herself now. "How dare you?"

Cody smacked it back even harder.

"One of those fucking things ATE her! What's the matter with you?"

Lauren's face broke, bursting into tears – infuriated by it, forcing them out all the harder.

Cody fell silent, subdued at the sight of a woman crying – making her even angrier.

The dock was approaching fast – a lonely pier used mostly by charter fishermen who wouldn't be returning for hours. Cody slowed abruptly, settling the boat down in the water.

Lauren said nothing, wiping her cheek angrily.

Cody glanced back at her, sullenly, as he guided the boat into the dock.

"Listen," he said finally – reluctantly, "I'm sorry."

He shifted awkwardly in his seat, as if uncomfortable with the concept.

But when he looked back at her, his eyes were genuine enough.

Although, Lauren thought archly, being 'genuine' was clearly not one of Cody Martin's big failings – there was never doubt he was speaking his true mind.

"I know," he said, as if agreeing with her thought, "I know... how I am."

His voice cracked ever-so-slightly.

"And I know you loved her too."

Lauren refused the recurring sting of tears.

Cody looked up at her helplessly. "It's just... I mean, I look at you – you're a friggin' twin sister – and it's just like I'm hearing her all over again."

Lauren said nothing. Cody bumped the boat into the dock, tossing a mooring rope, and pulling them in close. His earlier fit of temper seemed to have evaporated.

Mood swings, Lauren thought. Classic signs of grief.

Not that she was quite ready to forgive it yet.

Cody finished securing the boat, turning to her with a shrug.

"Well," he said, "I guess we're done here."

Lauren nodded, in perfect agreement for the first time.

Cody looked at her regretfully. "I'm sorry," he said again. "I just..."

He drifted off, letting the thought evaporate.

"Ah hell," he said. "I guess it doesn't matter now."

He looked back up at her.

"Listen," he said. "I'm hungry." He shrugged noncommittally. "You wanna get something to eat?"

He risked a quick smile.

"Someplace good this time," he said. "I'm buying."

CHAPTER 10

It was a little fish-shack right at the edge of the pier – surrounded by the token gift-shops that catered to the charter parties.

"This was her favorite place," Cody said as the hostess sat them at a table overlooking the ocean.

Lauren looked over the menu, and she could see why Carson had liked this place – in fact, it was a bit puzzling she had never mentioned it.

She did have a tendency to keep secrets. Lauren glanced up at Cody. Maybe this was a 'special place'.

It also might have been a guilty pleasure – Carson had a weakness for seafood – shellfish, in particular – it was, in fact, a vice that she and Lauren shared. And while every activist knew a seafood diet supported an industry that was depleting the oceans, they both occasionally justified the odd over-indulgence. They had once taken a party up to Alaska where they had gorged on giant king crab until they couldn't move.

Carson had evidently indulged a bit more than she had confided in her dear friend that she had.

The waitress smiled as she approached their table.

"Haven't seen you in a while," she said, pulling out her pad. "Can I get you some drinks to start?"

"Thanks, Annie," Cody said.

Annie nodded to Lauren. "The usual?" she asked.

Lauren blinked. "The usual?"

"Right," Annie said, apparently taking the question as a confirmation – she tucked her pad back in her pocket and turned for the kitchen. Lauren turned to Cody, doubtfully.

"I haven't been here in a while," Cody said. "She thinks you're Carson."

"Oh. What did I just order?"

He chuckled. "Her favorite."

"Uh oh." Lauren glanced back where Annie was already at the bar, pulling a series of high-octanes from the shelves. With a bartender's efficiency, she was back at their table in a moment, setting their drinks in front of them.

"Give you another minute to order?" she asked brightly – a waitress happy to see favored patrons.

Cody nodded, smiling and Annie retreated back to the kitchen.

Lauren took an experimental sip at her drink. She grimaced.

"Damn, that's stiff."

"Yeah," Cody agreed, "Long Island Ice Tea."

Lauren held the glass up, looking at the nearly clear fluid.

"Aren't they supposed to have some 'tea' in them?"

Cody nodded. "Yeah. That's why she liked them here. She had a tendency to let it all hang out."

Lauren took another tentative sip. There was certainly no doubt there. Ironically, that was probably something Cody had to find out after they had already met. Lauren smiled a little at the thought – Cody had probably never even seen Carson at a nightclub, where Lauren had spent more than one evening as a full-court-press babysitter. Those odd nights had been as hairy as anything they'd ever gotten into out on the ocean. The city cops knew their names just as well as the Coast Guard did.

"That's the funny thing," Cody said. "I was the old-lady of the two of us. I mean, I loved diving – even among big animals. But she was like, 'I'm gonna ride it'"

Lauren found herself smiling back – that was as good as she ever heard it said. For the first time, their eyes met, unguarded. At the crack of contact, Cody's smile faded, as the involuntary memory slapped a painful drop of happiness-gone-by across his face.

There was a moment of awkward silence.

Lauren eyed him cautiously. Was he looking at her 'like that'? She looked like Carson, after all.

Lauren wondered what was in his head. He seemed to prod his memories like a sore on the tongue – maybe a coping mechanism. She kept half-expecting him to start crying – she hoped he wouldn't, but she'd seen that sort of thing in otherwise macho-types before – suddenly getting all emotional – particularly in the presence of a woman.

She had also seen it used as a not-quite involuntary come-on.

But Cody wasn't even looking at her. As seemed to be his habit when trapped on land, when things got heavy, he turned to the ocean. A surfer riding it out.

For a moment, Lauren actually found herself seeing a bit of Carson in *him*.

The moment was broken by Annie, calling from the kitchen.

"You two ready yet?"

Lauren had debated just ordering a salad – a bit passive-aggressive. But the menu was just too tempting. And if today wasn't a reason to indulge, what was?

She ordered the jumbo shrimp and crab-leg combo, a side of chowder, and then, spotting a particular favorite under the appetizers, oyster shooters.

"I'll have three of those," she said.

Annie raised her eyebrows, "Really, honey?"

"Yeah," Cody said, "those are kinda high."

Lauren frowned. "Don't worry," she said, "I'll pay my own tab."

Cody shook his head. "That's not what I meant..."

But Annie was already waking away, scribbling on her pad. Cody shrugged.

That was another thing Lauren remembered Carson saying – he was always broke. Scattered employment at best – usually seasonal.

Lauren took another sip of her drink – she was already feeling a slight buzz – she would have to watch it. Cody said nothing, looking at her in that odd, speculative way. He took another sip of his own drink.

"So," Lauren said finally, "what's your 'usual'?"

He held up his glass. "Diet Coke."

"You don't drink? Why not?"

Cody smiled grimly. "Because I used to drink. My little incident with Carson's pre-med frat-boy wasn't my first brush with the law." He shrugged. "It's just best that I keep my inhibitions in place. The District Attorney's office agrees.

"But please," he said, indicating her own drink, "feel free to indulge."

He made a show of tossing his own glass of soda back as a shot. But the gesture held a heaviness to it, and as he spoke, his hand moved as if to cover his face.

"I never wanted her to see me like that, you know? Even after we split up, she... thought well of me. I didn't want that to ever change."

For the first time since she had met him, Cody seemed reluctant to meet her eye.

"The whole world could think I was a dirtbag, but not her."

Lauren nodded, wondering if he knew 'dirtbag' was one of hers, and one which she'd used a lot, back when they'd still been together – was he possibly giving her a subtle dig?

If so, his posture didn't show it – in fact, he seemed more self-loathing than anything.

"I know I didn't deserve her," he said. "I mean, she was only the greatest person I ever met."

He shook his head, brows furrowed, struggling to say it right.

"Right from the very second I saw her," he said. "I mean, a lot of girls in California are pretty. It was more than that. She... shined."

Lauren found herself nodding. Cody nodded back.

"Right?" he said. "It wasn't just me – it was everybody. It was like the rest of us were all leaves, and she was a sunlamp."

His lip wrinkled in that same involuntary smile. "It just *felt* good to be around her."

Lauren considered. She had never heard it put that way before, but now that she thought about it, it was true. That was Carson exactly.

Up until today, Cody had been an abstract character – and an adversarial one. It was bizarre listening to him talk about her best friend with an affection and familiarity as intimate as her own.

"See?" he said, "*everybody* loved her. The fact that I did too, didn't make me special."

The involuntary smile faltered at the pinprick of memory.

"What made me special," he said, "was that she liked me back."

Now it was Lauren's eyes that dropped – he would have known full-well Lauren herself had spent many a night trying to talk her out of that very thing.

But Cody's eyes weren't angry now, and his tone carried no accusation – and perhaps the subtle sting of his words were really more a by-product of the honest spoken truth.

"You'd never guess," Cody said, "that she was an LA princess by talking to her." He chuckled a little. "Although, I guess I should have figured it out just on her name alone. 'Carson Sheridan'. It sounds like a motel chain."

Lauren's own father was actually an investor in a national hotel chain, but she let it pass.

"But the hell of it," Cody continued, and now the crooked smile finally faded away, "whether she acted like it or not, she WAS a princess. And LA wasn't going to let me forget it. I figured that out the first time I took her home." He rolled his eyes. "Ever just been LOOKED at?"

"You know," he said, "really, up until that moment of my life, I thought I was just a regular guy. It wasn't until that exact moment I realized I was one of the undesirables – a 'surf bum'."

Lauren nodded sympathetically. 'Surf bum' was another one of hers. She hoped it didn't show on her face.

Cody blinked, looking right at her, and now he actually grinned. "Heh. Boy. *that's* your poker face?"

He shook his head. "Honey … Lauren..., I know you were one of them."

But his earlier temper was gone – his smile was good-natured and real.

"It's okay," he said. "It's what friends do."

He shrugged. "If it makes you feel any better, I know you were right. I know she went for someone better. Not just a better resume – a better 'catch'. Never once been arrested, I bet. He could give her a life I couldn't."

Lauren shifted uncomfortably in her seat. Another mirrored thought – although she still couldn't remember the guy's name, she remembered perfectly well her position at the time had been, 'if there's another option, take it'.

Cody nodded knowingly.

"It's okay," he said – again, as if reading her thoughts. He leaned back, his eyes turning reflective and thoughtful.

"You know," he said, "there was a minute there... where I think... I think.... I could have got her back. She called but I saw her number and... I just didn't pick up."

Cody stopped a moment, staring past her, considering, judging the truth of it.

With a heavy sigh, he nodded.

"Yeah," he said, "I think there was a moment there. But I let it pass. I let her go." He shook his head, as if wincing from the memory. "Best thing I could do for her, right?"

He fell silent.

Lauren had known Cody Martin for over two years, but less than a day – in that day, she had seen him stoic, mistrustful, and angry – and in retrospect, Lauren realized it was not so much an internal thing, as much as almost exclusively because of other people who had wanted nothing but to chase him away from someone he loved – even when he was paying his last respects.

But now, she thought she also saw flashes of the person Carson had seen.

Lauren herself felt a bit subdued – hearing her own opinion parroted from the perspective of someone who had been damaged by it.

"Letting her go," Cody continued, "was the hardest thing I've ever done."

Lauren remembered the point where Cody had finally stopped calling. Carson had sat by the phone for weeks, cat-nervous and mean, never once admitting it.

"You know how I got through it?" Cody asked, an ironic twitch touching his lips, as if embarrassed. "I told myself that maybe someday I'd make something of myself – that maybe someday I'd be... worthy."

He broke off abruptly.

"And now she's gone."

Cody fell silent, apparently finally running out of words.

Lauren sat quiet as well, twirling her straw in her drink. The ice was melting, so she simply took the rest of the glass in a swig.

She was actually a bit buzzier than she expected. But it was a fair enough night for a drink, she decided. She was already blowing her diet.

Besides, she would feel better once she ate something.

As if on cue, the kitchen door swung open and Annie appeared with their dinner orders, appetizers, and refilled Cody's coke – and sat another Long Island next to Lauren's empty glass.

Lauren glanced up at Cody. "I told you," he said, "she tended to let it all hang out."

Annie's eyes narrowed. "Is something wrong?"

"Actually," Cody said, "this isn't Carson. This is her friend, Lauren."

Annie looked nonplussed. "Oh," she said, "I'm so sorry." She stepped back taking a reappraising look at Lauren. "Wow. You're her friend? You could be sisters."

"So I'm told," Lauren said politely.

Annie glanced over at Cody – clearly wanting to ask more but, probably envisioning some sort of sordid love-triangle, chose discretion.

"Well," she said, unloading the rest of their dinner, "no charge for that Long Island, then."

She lined Lauren's oyster-shooters in a row behind her plateful of crab and shrimp, giving Lauren a little look as she did so.

Lauren eyed the second Long Island – she was already buzzy. Best to get something in her stomach, she thought, grabbing up the first of the oysters, dousing it with Tabasco, and tossing it down in a shot.

The metallic, salty taste was different somehow – perhaps the pepper in the sauce. She grabbed the second shooter and tossed that as well.

As she did so, she noted Cody looking at her oddly.

She found herself wondering what she was seeing – and how different it was from what Carson saw.

Lauren could see how an open-minded, non-judgmental person like Carson could be thrown by his type. He was good-looking, of course, and he was obviously intelligent – and on a normal day, was likely the typical, affable beach bum – just like they all were.

But intelligence was simply a raw trait – it did not preclude ignorance. And personality did not presuppose character.

He was an under-achiever, for sure. He never would have crossed into Lauren's own world, if not for his chance meeting with her best friend, through a shared hobby.

Yes, chemistry trumped social class, but only in the short-term. The world around inevitably imposes its strictures.

Of course, Lauren, herself, had been right there as an agent to enforce those strictures.

And as she looked at him now, the grief in his eyes was something different than what she had seen in Carson's pre-med frat-boy – whatever the hell his name was.

Besides simple pain, there was that self-loathing as well.

Did he blame himself for Carson's death? Because maybe he didn't try hard enough? Maybe because he wasn't there to protect her?

That would fit his personality type too.

Was he still trying to be worthy?

And was part of his frustration perhaps from being unable to bring her killer to justice?

A human murderer could be caught. But how do you find one fish in the sea?

Lauren wondered what he would say if she told him she actually could finger the specific shark that had sunk her boat – and the one that had most likely killed her.

The last text she had received from Carson was chillingly succinct.

"Big Rhonda just hit my boat. I'm sinking."

Lauren had not shown the message to anyone – specifically because Carson would not have wanted her to.

Identifying the attacker would ignite a lynch mob after it – and probably any other big shark in the area.

No matter what had happened, Lauren knew how Carson had lived her life, what her passions had been, and she wouldn't have wanted that.

Can't blame the shark.

And without a doubt, Cody would.

But perhaps, Lauren thought, he at least deserved a little peace.

"You know," she said, "if it helps – after you broke up – she was never with anyone else."

Cody blinked, looking up.

Lauren shrugged. "I mean, your pre-med frat-guy tried – that guy whose face you broke. But he was only around because her mother liked him. I never even met him. And she never talked about him at all."

She smiled a bit archly. "You, on the other hand, she wouldn't shut up about."

Cody absorbed this silently.

Lauren picked at the shrimp on her plate.

The buzzy feeling in her head was stronger now. That Long Island was really going to her head – she hadn't eaten a bite all day – she needed to get something more in her stomach. She grabbed up her last shooter.

As she tipped the glass, Cody started to raise his hand.

"You know you might want to slow down... oh hell, never mind."

Lauren tossed the oyster back. As she did so, the buzz in her head became a rush.

She realized she actually felt a bit wobbly. There was also that strange aftertaste.

"You know you took all three of those in less than ten minutes," Cody said. "On top of a Long Island."

Lauren rubbed her lips. "So?"

Cody eyed her. "You know there was a shot of hundred-proof vodka in each of those, don't you?"

Lauren blinked.

"Uh, no," she said. "Actually, I didn't."

She put her hand to her head. "Oh shit, I'm drunk."

Cody stared at her for a moment, deadpan.

Then he broke into open laughter.

"Oh boy, you really remind me of her, now." He picked up her empty shot glass. "That is exactly the sort of thing she would do."

Lauren put her hand to her head.

"Oh my God, that's not funny." She looked at him wide-eyed. "I'm serious – I don't drink like this."

"You gonna finish that second Long Island?"

Lauren glanced at the fresh glass. She had already taken a couple sips out of it.

She looked up at Cody helplessly. "Oh my God, what do I do? I'm going to be trashed."

Cody was still laughing. "Don't worry," he said, "I'll get you home. You might as well relax and ride it out."

He was trying to stop laughing, covering his face.

Then at the helpless look on her face – struggling to force back the incoming intoxication – he gave up and just laughed out loud.

Maybe it was the booze, but by the time he was done, Lauren was laughing right along with him. Annie glanced over in their direction, still wearing an uncertain look on her face.

When the laughter finally died out, they looked at each other, and relaxed for perhaps the first time.

"That actually felt kind of good," Cody said. "I think I needed that."

"Me too," Lauren said... only starting to slur.

She glanced over to her remaining drink – barely touched. She knew what Carson would do.

"Oh, what the hell," she said, picking it up and tossing it down.

"Alright," she said, "I think I'm drunk enough to take me home, now."

Cody grinned, waving a hand to Annie.

"Check," he said.

CHAPTER 11

The first thing Lauren was aware of the next morning, was waking up in her own bed. This was followed by a moment of relief, even if she was not quite sure how she got there.

A moment later, a heartbeat sent the thud of a hangover through her temples and she moaned aloud.

She blinked over bloodshot eyes, as fuzzy images from the night before began to trickle out of her subconscious.

Pretty much everything after the fish shack was a blur.

She really should not have taken that second Long Island.

Although it WAS what Carson would have done.

On the other hand, Carson would have pulled it better. Lauren remembered stumbling down the front steps into the parking lot outside the restaurant. She also remembered trying to give Cody directions as he drove her home – she specifically remembered messing these directions up at least twice, and pulling a map from under his dashboard – which she promptly used to get them good and lost. She further remembered Cody suggesting it was the navigator, not the map – to which she responded with frustrated blows to his arm and shoulder.

She knew she hit harder than she looked – harder than Cody was obviously expecting.

He rubbed his arm. "Damn. Ow."

It had been well after dark when they finally found Lauren's townhouse. Lauren had tangled her legs getting out of the old pickup and spilled herself out on to the driveway. She had fallen bonelessly, and so didn't hurt herself, but was still disoriented, and found it difficult to immediately get up.

Cody had looked down, shaking his head, before leaning over and grabbing her up, carrying her up the front steps.

"Of course, there's steps," he had muttered. "Why wouldn't there be steps?"

There had been a couple of hazardous moments off balance, hanging on his one arm, while he had fished her keys out of her purse. Then he had carried her inside, bumping off a couple of walls, before finding the lights, and setting her down on one of the kitchen chairs.

He had glanced around – the kitchen was spotless. As was the rest of the townhouse. Not a loose shoe, nor stray glass or dish. Cody smiled a little, shaking his head.

"You're laughing at me," Lauren accused.

"No," he said.... laughing. "It's just... boy, are you just like her. For a supposedly free spirit, she had a strong streak of anal-retentive control-freak."

Lauren frowned, just a touch belligerent. "I never saw her as a control-freak."

Cody had laughed. "Oh, *hell* yeah. What do you think 'I'm gonna ride him', is all about?"

Lauren had paused on that – a moment of sober clarity – it was perhaps more astute than she would have given him credit for.

With that, he hiked her up again, and carried her back to her bedroom, setting her gently on the perfectly-made bed.

"Okay, Princess," he said. "Time to call it a night."

She had been very dozy at this point, feeling her eyelids start to flutter as she lay back on her clean sheets.

She remembered Cody smiling indulgently, down at her as she settled in. Then she remembered making the odd comment, "You know, you really are a pretty nice guy."

After that...

Well, she really couldn't remember much at all.

She must have simply fallen asleep.

Sitting up for the first time, Lauren did a quick survey of her room, checking herself under the sheets – a t-shirt and panties.

Then she realized the water was running – from down the hall – someone in the shower.

Lauren's heart skipped a beat as the water turned off and, after a moment, Cody stepped into the hall. He was wearing one of her robes.

He smiled as he tapped on the open door to her bedroom.

"Morning sunshine," he said. "And how are we feeling today?"

"Oh my God," Lauren said, covering her face. "Oh my God. Oh no."

Cody's head cocked. "Something wrong?"

Lauren pulled at her hair. "Is something wrong? Oh my God, are you kidding? Did we just sleep together?"

Cody shrugged. "I guess technically – you were pretty drunk."

Lauren threw a pillow at him. "Oh my God, you are such a pig!"

He brows furrowed. "Now hold on a second..."

But Lauren wasn't trying to listen.

"Doesn't this bother you?" she said.

Cody shrugged, standing there in her robe.

"No. Not really."

"And what do you think you'd say to Carson if she knew you'd slept with her best friend?"

Cody considered. "I guess I'd tell her maybe you weren't her best friend after all."

Lauren remembered the thunderstruck way Carson said he could piss you off.

For a moment, she literally sputtered.

Cody took the opportunity to retreat back to the shower, dressing quickly, and returning from the kitchen with a cup of freshly brewed coffee and a couple aspirin.

"Here," he said, "this'll help."

Lauren simmered silently, but she did take the offered aspirin.

"Listen," Cody said, as if everything were perfectly fine, "you're upset. I think I'm just going to leave." But he held up his phone.

"I took the liberty of dialing my number on your phone, so you can get hold of me if you need to."

"Why in God's name would I need to get hold of you?'"

"Well," he said, holding up his own phone, "I also took the liberty of forwarding these pictures you took to my own phone. Dead whale, seals. The whole bit. I'm going to give you a week with your academic eco-nut friends to make a 'responsible' statement about the situation here, and then I'm going to go to the press myself."

Lauren blinked, sitting up quickly.

"Are you kidding me?" Lauren reached for his phone, but he pulled back.

"One week," he said, "for you to do the right thing."

Ignoring her pounding head, Lauren followed him down the hall, catching him at the front door.

"Wait a minute," she said angrily. "Are you really this big a jerk?"

He shrugged. "I guess so."

His eyes narrowed. "You know, I'm a little moral-torn myself, here. If someone else gets killed because I let you sit on this for a week, it'll be my fault too."

Lauren said nothing, glaring.

Brushing past her, Cody opened the door and let himself out, fishing in his pocket for his keys. But then he paused, glancing back over his shoulder, as if considering.

Lauren stood in the doorway. "What? What do you want?"

He sighed. "If it makes you feel any better, nothing happened last night." He shrugged. "You were drunk."

Lauren blinked. "Nothing?"

"I slept next to you after you passed out. You were talking for a while. That's what I was trying to tell you."

"Oh." Lauren cleared her voice. "I'm sorry."

Cody shrugged, smiling, turning to leave. "Don't worry about it," he said.

As he did so, Lauren noticed a mark on his neck.

She leaned forward. "Is... that a hickey?"

Cody touched a hand to his neck.

"Oh. Yeah." He shrugged again. "What can I say? It took me a minute to decide you were too drunk."

He ducked as Lauren threw the full cup of coffee over his head.

"You ASSHOLE!"

She slammed the door behind her.

Pulling at her shirt, she inspected her body for odd marks – or possibly a reciprocal hickey or two – quivering at the thought. All she wanted now was to shower and scrub.... except the shower was still full of steam – as well as his musky man smell – with his wet footprints still on the floor.

Lauren sat down on the couch, cringing in self-disgust, her hangover pounding away.

The part of her that was not her friend reminded her that SHE apparently had given HIM the hickey.

"Oh, I'm gonna be sick."

Her voice was a low moan.

By definition, that not only meant she had come on to HIM, but HE had taken the moral high-road by turning her down.

Lauren wondered if Carson had ever been turned down in her life – drunk or not drunk.

In a bizarre way, Lauren felt somehow insulted.

Worse, she was humiliated. As if she were some pathetic kid sister.

Even worse than that, he had actually tried to be nice about it, before she had blown up in his face.

Yep. She was pretty much looking bad on all fronts.

She hiked her knees up to her chest, hugging them against her, curling into a ball on the couch.

It wasn't her fault. She didn't intend to get drunk.

Well..., not THAT drunk. She had taken on two Long Islands.

Now, all that was left was to spend the day laying in the dark with the curtains closed, swearing to never drink again.

Pulling a pillow over her head, she set to do just that.

At that moment, there was a knock at the door.

Lauren glared with bloody eyes. Cody couldn't really be coming back, could he?

She got ready to be pissed again. She got up, wondering if she was still willing to even let him in, uncertain if the guiding emotion was anger, shame, or pride.

Having no idea what she was going to say, Lauren opened the door.

But it wasn't Cody.

Lauren recognized the slight-framed man with the goatee, who had approached Cody after the service. The reporter.

"Excuse me, Miss... Palmer, is it? Lauren Palmer?"

Lauren nodded slowly, suddenly aware of her slight dress, stepping more fully behind the door.

"I'm sorry to disturb you," he said, "but my name is David Templeton. I'm a reporter. I was wondering if I could talk to you for a few minutes?"

Lauren studied the man's face – a bit rat-like, she thought.

"What's this about?" Lauren asked.

David Templeton smiled.

"I have a proposition for you," he said.

CHAPTER 12

Lauren was beginning to have second thoughts.

It had not even been a week since she'd last been out on the ocean. At one time, that would have been a trial in itself – a punishment, even.

Today was different.

Behind, lay Surf Shore. Ahead, lay the rocky cove that had concealed the burgeoning seal colony.

Cody had been right. The place just *felt* dangerous.

So, part of the edginess was exactly that.

Then, of course, there was David Templeton.

Lauren thought again of those interior warning signals that supposedly evolved humans consistently ignored.

"Call me Dave," he had said. In another person, that would have been familiarity. In David Templeton's case, it was a sale's pitch.

Still, so far, at least, he had been as good as his word. He had, in fact, actually managed to procure the very same boat Lauren had used on loan with her student crew – already with a cage hook-up and everything.

Today, the boat was piloted by the charter captain who owned it – a guy named Mundus who ran a commercial shark-cage-diving operation – usually out of the Sea of Cortes – but was willing to loan his boat out during the off-season.

It was a sturdy-enough craft. And up until just last week, she had felt quite confident as a passenger, even in water populated by big Great Whites.

Of course, hadn't the premise of that illusion of safety – be it in the cage, in the boat... all of it – hadn't that always been pretty much based on the general idea that the sharks *wouldn't* go after them? Simply because they were bigger than the sharks were?

And while it was a bigger boat than the last time she'd dared these waters, it was not a *lot* bigger.

And end-to-end, it was still smaller than that whale.

Lauren glanced up where Captain Mundus guided them through the choppy water. She had never met him, but knew his reputation – certainly a competent-enough captain, who had a lot of experience with sharks. He was also clearly used to dealing with tourists, as opposed to professional researchers. It was also a privatized business that Lauren rather disapproved of – exploitative and invasive, without the considerations of her own academic-funded dives.

The rest of the crew consisted of Mundus' mate – an Australian-sounding guy named Mike – and David Templeton's camera man, Matt – a tall skinny guy with deliberately scruffy hair and dress, who carried his camcorder on his shoulder like a parrot. Lauren found herself looking at the camera self-consciously.

How different it was than spending time on the ocean with her grad-student crew. There was something... industrial about it. It was work versus recreation.

Lauren watched Captain Mundus' mechanical moves behind the wheel.

There was no magic in the ocean for Captain Frank Mundus – it was the equivalent of a factory job – hard, smelly, dangerous work. Both Mundus and his mate bore the weathered, corded arms of a lifetime of hard labor.

David Templeton on the other hand, was clearly enjoying himself.

As the trip was his charter, he seemed to perceive himself as 'leader'.

While, to his credit, he had surrounded himself with experts – both in sharks and in boats – Lauren couldn't help but notice the difference between a journalist and a producer – a journalist simply would have filmed it all; a producer wanted to manage it – with the added wrinkle that he also apparently intended to star in it.

He claimed to have experience scuba-diving – which from what Lauren could ascertain, meant a couple of vacations in Hawaii.

Then there was the moment he produced from his pack a large speargun.

"What exactly is that for?" Lauren had asked.

Templeton had given her a look. "What do you think?"

"You realize Great Whites are protected animals, don't you?"

Templeton had smiled ironically. "Well, that's kind of the point of our little production, isn't it?" He hefted the speargun over his shoulder. "Don't worry. I won't poke it at any of your precious sharks unless they come after me first."

Lauren had also noticed that, as he exchanged narrative banter with Matt the cameraman – who followed him with his single-hand recorder – Templeton managed to do so as much as possible with Lauren herself in the frame. He had made a joking reference to 'eye-candy'.

Matt, being the mostly amiable sort – obviously used to dealing with David Templeton – had complied readily enough. Lauren was dressed in her customary diving gear – her bikini bottoms and scuba vest – basically the same outfit she'd sported in countless online videos, not to mention public beaches – yet here she felt ridiculously exploited and exposed.

Perhaps it was a bit of karma – before coming out here today (and feeling a bit evil for it), Lauren had sent a text to Cody, informing him she was not only going to the press, but David Templeton.

Cody had not responded right away, and Lauren smiled at the thought of his expression on the other end.

His follow-up text was typically succinct. "You've got two days," it said. "And tell David Templeton I said to go fuck himself."

Lauren had shown the message to David Templeton, who had smiled indulgently.

"Mr. Martin doesn't like me much," he had told her that day at her doorstep.

Lauren had snatched up the robe Cody had abandoned, but stayed behind her door.

"Actually, he says you're a sensationalist hack."

David Templeton had smiled.

"That's because he committed an assault, which is a crime, and he didn't like it being reported."

Lauren had crooked her head. "Assault like poking someone in the chest?"

Templeton had smiled. "To be fair, he didn't give me a chance to speak. I was actually offering him a chance at redemption." Templeton shrugged. "I pretty much got my answer from him yesterday. Now I'm asking you."

"You're asking me what?"

David Templeton smiled. "I think your friend Cody is right."

My 'friend', now, Lauren thought. "Right about what?"

Templeton folded his hands.

"I believe that, because of over-extended conservation policies, the California coast has become overpopulated with white sharks. Your best friend, Carson Sheridan – who also happened to be the daughter of one of my editor's best friends – was recently killed because of that.

"The point of my piece," Templeton said, "is that the ban on fishing for white sharks be lifted and their endangered status be revoked. "

Lauren's hangover had already been pounding. Now a throb of temper cranked the pulse in her ears just a little louder.

"Cody was right about one thing," she said. "You are a hack. Just because a species rebounds after nearly being exterminated doesn't mean it's over-populated."

"They're definitely over-populated for a human environment. People are being killed."

"More people are killed in cars," Lauren said. "You want to ban those?"

Templeton smiled. "Well, we are in California."

"You can't blame the sharks for human encroachment. This is all about human interference with nature. They're part of the ecosystem. They're the apex predator."

"Ah," Templeton said, raising a finger as if waiting on that point, "why do you need an apex predator in a human-environment?" He smiled. "That's *our* job."

Lauren started to respond, before remembering she was talking to the press. She was about to answer with something about humans as invasive species, and not having a right to the whole planet, before remembering how that could be spun.

What had Cody said? Eco-nuts who put the lives of fish before humans?

But Templeton had held up a placating hand.

"Look," he said, "what I want is to put you on camera."

Lauren shook her head, amazed. "Why would I possibly agree to that?"

"Because," Templeton said, "then you would have the opportunity to present your own view. Your counter point." He shrugged. "I'm going to put my point of view out there whether you have your say or not."

Lauren's eyes narrowed.

"So why come to me at all?"

"For the same reason I approached Cody Martin, yesterday," he said.

Templeton leaned forward. Lauren faded slightly behind her door.

"I need you to take me out there."

Lauren frowned. "Out there, where?"

Templeton smiled. "Out to where you and Mr. Martin went yesterday."

Lauren said nothing. What exactly did this guy know? Or what did he suspect? He was a reporter, after all. He had apparently been watching them closely enough to know where she lived. Certainly, enough to have seen Cody leave.

Did he know about the seal colony?

Templeton had smiled disarmingly.

"Look," he said, "here's my card. I'm setting up a charter in three days. Let me know if you want on board."

Lauren had accepted his card, saying nothing more, watching until he got in his car and drove away before shutting the door.

Two-days later, the night before the trip, she had called him and agreed to go.

And now, as Captain Mundus guided them through the choppy water, the twin rocky peninsulas loomed ahead.

Lauren had already done her direct interview – filmed as they had passed Surf Shore, with the coast in the background over her shoulder. She'd done her whole schpeel about the ecology and the public's irrational fear of sharks, and respect for the ocean and nature – and yadda-yadda-yadda – and found herself feeling frustrated.

Her words sounded hollow as she spoke – standard activist bumper sticker fare.

Never in her life had she been able to properly express why she believed so strongly in her purpose. How do you explain the spiritual?

It also reflected what Lauren had always believed to be an unfailing fallacy of humankind – to destroy what makes them afraid. It was a hold-back from when we were all nothing but apes – using our newly-evolved minds to join together against larger, more dangerous animals – translating that instinct through modern humanity, and you wiped whole species from the planet.

How much less destructive could we all be, if we just took time to understand?

Lauren had seen no human population – no country, people, or demographic – that was immune to that depredation of the human animal.

In a nutshell, that was why she was here today – in her own small way, she was standing against fear and the destruction that always followed.

Just right now, however, Lauren was not so sure she was accomplishing that.

David Templeton was pointing just ahead as they cruised the point.

"Look!" he was shouting excitedly. "There's something out there."

Captain Mundus shaded the sun from his eyes – checking out the horizon with a pair of binoculars.

"Well, I'll be..."

Mundus shifted gears, dropping down into neutral, steering as their momentum carried them forward.

There was a large mass floating in the water ahead. Lauren had brought a pair of her own binoculars, and raised them to her eyes, expecting to see the same deteriorating whale carcass from earlier in the week.

But it wasn't.

It was an orca. A ten-foot calf.

Floating, with several large bites taken from it – the first one right near the base of the tail.

CHAPTER 13

Captain Mundus pulled them up beside the baby orca. First mate Mike hooked the carcass with a gaff, pulling it in close.

Matt the cameraman panned in.

David Templeton raised a reporter's eye to Lauren. "Well, Miss Palmer?" he said.

But Lauren was struck dumb. The import of what she was seeing was only just beginning to register. This was more than just a large target being hit.

This was an orca – a calf, no less.

In ecological terms, this was an act of war.

Orca mamas took this sort of thing personally.

Captain Mundus pulled the calf in next to the boat, pulling a rope around the tail, and winching the carcass partially out of the water.

The bites were massive. Lauren shook her head. That *had* to have been Rhonda. There were only a few besides her that it *could* be.

But this was unprecedented aggression. Could it be a shark as big as Rhonda would become bold enough to engage orcas directly?

There was a caste-system in white shark prey as they grew. Smaller whites fed on fish. But as their calorie requirements grew, they began to focus on seals.

There hadn't been sharks big enough to target whales since Megalodon.

But perhaps, after they grew to a certain size...?

And not just a whale – an orca. Granted, it was a small one and, really, *any* big white could theoretically take a calf of this size.

The fact that it *did*, however, challenged the very hierarchy of the ocean.

"I've seen a lot of orcas this year," Mundus was saying. "More than one large pod has been touring the coasts."

"The white sharks are gone from the Farallons this year," Lauren volunteered.

Mundus nodded. "Sometimes the transient seal-hunting pods will circle through there. That would drive the sharks out."

David Templeton reached over the edge to touch one of the massive wounds on the dead whale calf.

"The Farallons are sixty miles north," he said. "Where did this little guy come from?"

"Well," Mundus said, "the thing about orcas is that they're tribal – they got different habits, and they hunt different prey. Some hunt seals. Some hunt whales, or squid, or penguins. And some hunt sharks. And the tribes don't mingle."

Lauren was nodding.

"And if a seal-hunting pod drove the sharks out of the Farallons," she said, "it would stand to reason that a shark-hunter pod would follow them."

Lauren looked out over the water. They actually hadn't seen any orcas all day – had this little guy got separated from his pod somehow? Calves usually didn't stray far from their mothers. Perhaps it was just an adventurous juvenile?

It followed, a moment later, for her to wonder that the kill had been abandoned.

Whale carcasses of all kinds were white shark feasts – especially around here, at this time of year. Why not this one?

Had the mother been around, Lauren wondered? If so. Where had she gone? Had she actually been driven off by the shark?

Could this have even been a territorial attack aimed at the orcas themselves?

Was such a thing possible? It was amazing how often instinct seemed to almost mimic strategic thought.

In any case, it was enough to challenge her own beliefs on the subject.

As she looked around at the deceptively empty water, she also took quiet note that the baby whale was a fresh kill.

As such, there was also the rather likely possibility that the carcass had not actually been abandoned and that, even now, the killer lurked, hidden in the dimness not so very far below.

David Templeton was smiling.

"What do you think, Miss Palmer?" he said. "Ready for a dive?"

He tapped the metal bars of the shark cage where it was lashed to the deck.

"That's why we're here, right?" Templeton looked at her expectantly.

Lauren didn't answer right away.

If this animal was becoming *this* bold and aggressive...

First mate Mike let the winch loose, dropping the dead orca back into the water. The boat bobbed up and down in relief.

Mike looked down at the surrounding surface.

"There don't seem to be any sharks around to dive with," he said.

"Oh, they're out there, alright," Captain Mundus said. "We probably scattered them when we showed up."

Lauren nodded. "They won't be far off."

She looked over the side where the water turned dark. This was where the ocean dropped off. It was actually much deeper here than it seemed this near the coast – sort of an offshore canyon – perhaps even a crevice – running along the beach. In the same way the broken peninsula had provided haven for the congregating seals, so did the broken shelf grant a haven for the sharks – they could go down deep.

A place to flee to, Lauren thought, if, say, they had just pissed off a mother orca, and hide until her grieving pod had gone.

But Captain Mundus was right. They were out there.

There was a shadow visible beneath the surface – right where the shelf broke away at the edge of the trench – the deep open water beyond, despite appearances, was not empty.

David Templeton, however, was not inclined to patience. "Maybe we should throw out some fish guts or something."

Lauren indicated the dead whale. "This by itself ought to be enough."

Templeton turned his head up to Captain Mundus, who shrugged, nodding to first-mate, Mike. There were several buckets tied to the railing and Mike grabbed up one of these, peeling the lid and releasing the noxious aroma of blood and chum.

Matt the cameraman made the mistake of leaning in too close with his camera and caught a full breath of the gagging stench.

"Oh, good Lord," he gasped. "That's disgusting."

Mike shrugged. "Old chum," he said. "Been sitting in buckets since our last charter." Mike smiled. "Fermentation. Gives it a little extra spice."

Lauren covered her own nose as well. There was no doubt the scent would carry quickly underwater.

Mike dipped a ladle into the smelly mix and tossed a glut out over the water in the direction of the floating orca carcass.

But before the first splatter hit the water, something hit the little whale from below.

CHAPTER 14

It was Rhonda, all right.

As the orca calf's carcass settled with the wave, Lauren could see her massive snout with its tell-tale markings, latched onto the little whale's side, carving out a massive chunk of blubber

Rhonda wasn't alone either. A moment later, as if arriving in a school, several more fins appeared, all circling inward, giving Rhonda plenty of room before moving in to take bites of their own.

Lauren recognized the marked fin of Mack the Knife, as well as several other regulars she normally associated with the Farallons this time of year.

These were all large adults. Lauren was working a bit of retroactive algebra as she counted fins.

Up until now, they had always assumed the Farallons were the primary feeding point along the California migratory route – thus the sheer number of sharks in that area had not seemed alarming – not overpopulation – just a healthy robust community.

If, however, this new seal colony was becoming a bleed off of the Farallons, then suddenly you were looking at potentially supporting half again or more.

And if Captain Mundus was right about the seal-hunting orca pods driving the whites out of the Farallons, then you had forced congestion of big, hungry, likely territorial adults, of both sexes, all crammed into an environment that typically supported – what – a third or a quarter of that number?

A tempest in a teapot, for sure.

It also meant, Lauren found herself admitting reluctantly, that Cody Martin, in a large part, had been right.

"Hey," Matt said from behind her, "check *this* one out!"

They all turned where Matt was filming off the opposite side of the boat.

A single large fin, solitary and subtle, glided in discretely from their rear.

Bloody Mary, Lauren thought. Always coming in from behind you.

Mary passed smoothly under their boat, and Lauren could feel the swell beneath her feet as the boat was lifted easily in the water.

Older, sneakier, and every bit as big as Rhonda.

Twenty foot – six meters – was always the toss-off estimate for big sharks – crocs too, Lauren had noticed. Something about that magic number – it didn't matter – the press, fishermen, all the online blogs.

Lauren didn't think she would make that estimate lightly ever again.

As big as a sixteen-footer might appear, once you've seen a real twenty-footer, there was no mistaking the difference. And now there were two of them, circling beneath their feet. Not to mention a host of big adults that ranged comfortably into the sixteen to eighteen-foot range themselves.

David Templeton looked doubtful for the first time.

"These are some BIG sharks," he said, looking down as Rhonda herself cruised slowly passed the stern.

Lauren pointed. "Well, there's your star," she said. "If you're looking for a celebrity, she's the queen. The biggest shark in the area, with lots of attitude."

"Big Rhonda," Templeton said, smiling at her. "I've seen your videos, Miss Palmer."

He nodded to Matt. "She's right," he told him. "Keep your camera on that one."

Templeton opened his own camera bag – a specialty underwater model with an attachment to fit comfortably on one's shoulder.

"Well, Miss Palmer," he said. "Do you think anyone's ever filmed two twenty-footers from a cage at the same time before?"

Lauren allowed that it was not likely.

Within minutes, they were setting up the cage.

CHAPTER 15

Lauren had dressed down for diving herself – it had been why she had come, after all. It was hardly the first time she had cage-dived. She had even done free-diving with sharks.

Although not with Great Whites.

Not like Carson.

Lauren found herself staring over the railing at the cadre of fins circling around the little whale carcass as Captain Mundus and first-mate Mike lifted the cage over the side.

As they did so, one of the fins veered in their direction. There was a loud clang as the metal cage was knocked beneath the surface into the stern – and none too gently either.

The impact rocked the boat, prompting laughter from Captain Mundus, and a startled, "Holy shit!" from Matt, who had been leaning in close with his camera.

David Templeton had leaned over with his own shoulder cam, following the recalcitrant shark as it circled the foreign object dangling off the side of the boat. He laughed nervously. Beside him, Mike looked somewhat less confident than his captain, as he checked the cage's moorings.

Mundus flipped the top of the cage open, glancing over his shoulder where Lauren stood hesitantly.

"Well, Miss," Mundus said. "You're up."

Lauren had already shouldered up her air tank, but now she found herself shaking her head.

In fact, the hairs on her neck were curling with that same instinctive sense of dread – one of those interior warnings that human beings seemed so often to ignore.

"Something's wrong, here," she said.

David Templeton was suited up with his own air tank. He frowned.

"What do you mean 'wrong'?"

Lauren was shaking her head, pulling at the straps on her tank.

"They're too agitated," she said. "I've never been around this many big ones."

"You also told me no one's ever filmed anything like it either." Templeton shrugged. "I mean the cages are safe, right?"

Captain Mundus smiled indulgently. "We haven't lost anybody yet."

There was a heartbeat where the word 'yet' seemed to hang on the air a bit longer than it should. It was probably intended as tension-relieving levity.

Around here, however, that just didn't work.

"The thing is," Lauren said, "these cages are designed on the principle that these sharks won't be launching an all-out attack on a non-prey item."

Mundus rapped his knuckles on the metal bars.

"They aren't biting through this," he said.

"Maybe not," Lauren replied. "But I had one hit a cage hard enough to bend them. Right up the coast from here in fact."

David Templeton glanced over the side at the circling fins, and then back at the cage floating in the water.

"There was also," Lauren continued, "a case where a medium-sized white slipped in between bars of a cage at the attachment points, and tore it open from the inside."

"This is a hell of a time to mention *that*," Templeton said.

"This trip was your idea," Lauren answered.

Templeton turned back to Mundus, who shrugged.

"There's never been a cage-diver killed by a shark," he said. "That one case where the cage broke open, the diver escaped safely to the boat."

"He wasn't swimming in water like this," Lauren said. She turned to Templeton. "You want my professional advice, there it is. It's not safe. Not here. Not today."

Lauren shook her head.

"Let me put it this way," she said, "*I'm* not going down there."

Templeton looked over at Mundus doubtfully. Mundus shrugged. "It's your charter," the Captain said. "It's up to you."

There was another thump as something from below knocked against the cage again. Templeton's eyes widened.

Then he glanced back at Matt the cameraman, apparently remembering he was being recorded, and adjusted his posture accordingly.

"Well," he said, with just a touch of forced bravado, "no guts no glory." He smiled deliberately. "After all, no one's ever died BEFORE, right?"

Lauren could see he was talking himself into it. Another human ignoring those survival instincts. Still, she tried anyway.

"There are," she said, "a lot of things going on out here that haven't ever happened before."

Templeton hefted his speargun. "Well," he said, "that's why I brought this."

Lauren frowned.

Behind him, there was yet another bump from below, knocking the cage against the boat.

Captain Mundus raised his eyebrows. "They are pretty squirrelly today."

Templeton's affected expression of confidence faltered just a little bit. But he pushed it back. He probably considered it courage.

Lauren herself, had noted a consistent difference between courageous and foolhardy.

With a deliberate eye towards the camera, Templeton winked nonchalantly.

"Okay," he said, "let's do it."

CHAPTER 16

David Templeton didn't look it, but he had done a lot of daredevil things in his life – he had once done a feature on bungee-jumping, that ended with a highlight of himself diving off a bridge with a head-cam. The point, he believed, was to trust the equipment and the technology, and always surround yourself with professionals. Thus, in reality, he consciously knew he was not statistically taking any more risk than someone flying a commercial airliner, or riding a taxi. The risk was simply a state of mind.

As it turned out, while his scuba experience consisted of exactly two four-hour classes on separate vacations, the mechanics of today's 'dive', as he saw it, was no more complicated than dipping ten feet down in a pool – he wouldn't even have to worry about coming up slowly.

He was also confident in the strength of the cage. He had briefly looked up the incident Lauren had cited, and had determined that was simply a case of a breakaway design on the cage – intended to make it lightweight – that had revealed that particular structural flaw when the shark inadvertently wedged itself between the bars and leveraged the whole thing apart.

Also, it was a small shark – small enough to fit its snout between two bars.

Not a problem today.

These sharks were WAY too big for that.

Captain Mundus was smiling, holding the hatch open expectantly.

With a quick look around the surface, scouting for errant, prowling fins, Templeton slipped his legs over the railing, and slid down into the cage.

Once inside, he pulled on his mask and mouthpiece, taking a few test breaths and blowing bubbles before giving a thumbs up.

Mundus slammed the lid on the cage shut. It made the satisfactorily loud clang of reinforced steel.

Then there was the audible crank of the winch as they lowered him below the surface.

The water was surprisingly cold – it was a drop-off point into open ocean, but his wet-suit kept him comfortably warm – he also always spent his budget on top notch equipment.

Just like the speargun in his hands.

Templeton peered into the gray-blue water.

The one thing he remembered most vividly about his scuba trips in the tropics, was the weird, trippy feeling of being – of breathing – underwater – the odd cast of light, and the brilliant CGI-like fish and colors that fairly danced around you – combined with that feeling of floating – of flying – a fully three-dimensional world where your every movement was propulsion.

Templeton could understand how people could get addicted to it.

This, however, was nothing like that at all.

First of all, he was in a cage – the graceful feeling of movement was completely absent, replaced by a rather claustrophobic feeling of being trapped underwater.

Then there was the surrounding water. To the east, was nothing but pure unending blue, descending into darkness. Behind him, was the crest of rocky shelf. The Disney-like fauna was not in evidence along this inhospitable bit of coast.

Templeton turned the camera on his shoulder towards the floating baby orca, which from below, was simply a large floating mass. Mundus had cut the carcass loose, and now it was floating several yards away from the boat.

For the moment, the water around it was empty.

He had read that Great Whites could be skittish – perhaps dropping the cage had scared them off.

Then, from just below, ascending as if materializing out of mist, was the first of a number of cruising shadows that hovered just beyond the reach of sight.

In another moment, the boldest of them circled in for a view.

Templeton raised the camera as they passed his cage, a couple of them bumping the bars interestedly along the way. That's what the noises had been – not one shark, but several swimming by.

As he followed them with his camera, he realized they were really after the baby whale – over a ton of easily available meat and blubber.

His cage continued to be bumped in procession – Templeton was surprised at how many sharks there actually were – it was hard to tell as they circled in and out of sight, but he counted at least six, maybe seven or more, different individuals at once. All fifteen-feet or better.

And as he watched them, Templeton thought he understood something about people like Lauren Palmer and Carson Sheridan – why they would LIKE an animal like this.

Underwater, they appeared very different. Rather than the smashing jaws visible from above as they mauled and cannibalized a whale carcass, down here, they were graceful and rather serene. And as they gathered underneath the floating whale, they looked a bit like a line of piglets, all suckling from their mother.

Then, all at once, almost as a flock, the group of them abandoned the trough, falling away and scattering into the surrounding gloom.

Templeton followed the last of them as they disappeared into that perfect haze of light that made them all but invisible.

He kept his camera focused below. For several minutes there was nothing but darkness.

Then the reason for the other sharks' flight came drifting up out of the darkness.

Templeton zoomed the frame back. It was one of the largest sharks he'd seen – the one Lauren called 'Big Rhonda'.

Estimated at twenty feet.

And Templeton was willing to put her at every bit of that.

She made her initial pass alongside the cage and boat, inspecting the carcass she'd left behind. From beneath, Templeton saw one of the other sharks lingering hopefully at the periphery, whereupon Rhonda abruptly turned on it, her fins posturing, coming up at the upstart shark from below, snapping at its gills. The smaller shark thrashed in retreat, and just beyond the range of vision, Templeton saw a rush of other cruising shadows quickly ceding ground, leaving Rhonda, for the moment, circling alone.

Now, she turned her attention back to him.

The big shark had already made several passes and several bumps at the strange new object in her territory – a foreign anomaly apparently associated with the larger object floating above. She had so far shown no particular interest in either, although she had mouthed the bars of the cage experimentally.

His heart pounding, remembering to control his breathing and not use up his air, Templeton aimed the camera down the gaping throat as the mouth mawed less than two-feet in front of him

As he did so, he decided he had been wrong before. This WAS different than flying commercial.

The five-thousand-pound animal hung lazily for a moment, its jaws locked over two bars approximately three-feet apart, gnawing, testing the strength. Templeton tried to remember the latest numbers from studies of white shark bites. A couple of tons-plus bite force? Something like that? Behind two-inch teeth?

He found himself looking down at the speargun strapped to his wrist.

While safely standing on the boat, the barbed-shaft had seemed really nasty-looking. Looking back up at the mass of muscle gnawing so casually at his metal refuge, and suddenly it seemed about as threatening as a toothpick.

Rhonda shook the cage slowly back and forth – not hard – simply mouthing for something that would bite off.

Then, apparently giving up, she turned to investigate the boat itself.

Templeton could see the others looking down through the water, although the rolling surface distorted their faces. But he could see definite movement on board as Rhonda made several exploratory bumps from below their feet.

The shark was nearly the length of the boat. Templeton raised his camera, following her as she passed back and forth.

Then, abruptly, Big Rhonda veered off, making a quick pass by the whale carcass, as if for a spot-check, before disappearing into the misty blue just as the others had.

Templeton looked around at the apparently empty ocean. Long minutes passed.

Were they done for the day?

He turned back up, looking for the boat, and was changing the focus on his camera when Rhonda suddenly reappeared, rocketing up from below, striking the stern of the boat not ten feet above him. Templeton felt the rushing swell shoving him against the back of the cage. There was a crunching 'crack' that reverberated through the water, and he felt his cage suddenly drop nearly ten feet deeper.

Templeton blinked. He could clearly see the winch arm had dropped and was now dangling out over the water.

He could also see a gaping hole bitten into the boat's stern – the strike had hit just high of the motor, which now hung loose.

Like hitting the tail of a whale, Templeton thought.

In another rush of movement, again from below, Rhonda struck again, hitting the same spot, tearing the motor completely away. Templeton could see the stern dipping below the surface.

The cage dropped another dozen feet.

"Oh my God," he breathed.

Above him, he saw kicking legs as the crew was dumped into the water.

Around him, the cage began to descend, pulling the boat down with it, leaving the swimmers on the surface.

As his cage dropped into the darkness, Templeton saw Rhonda circling above.

CHAPTER 17

Lauren couldn't believe it. It was like standing still and watching a fist coming at you in slow-motion, yet being unable to move out of the way.

The first hit from below knocked them all off their feet. Matt the cameraman had blurted unintelligible profanity. Captain Mundus had nearly fallen overboard, while Mike had grabbed hold of the cabin door, which promptly sprung open and he tumbled roughly into the stern railing, just as water began rushing in where the motor had been torn loose.

There was a brief stunned pause, as they all stared at the incoming ocean, before they were hit again.

This blow simply dropped the motor off the back of the boat, leaving a gaping hole. The boat dipped sharply to its stern, nearly setting them upright in the water.

There was one dizzying moment before gravity caught and slid them down the smooth deck into the water.

At the first strike, Lauren had made a move towards the cabin – her first instinctive thought had been the radio – but as Mike had yanked the door open, as he'd lost his footing, Lauren now found herself clinging to the knob.

With the water bubbling beneath her, she pulled her way into the cabin itself, even as the three men below her were dropped into the ocean.

The boat itself was following rapidly. In a moment, the deck was under the surface, the boat momentarily bobbing at the air pocket within. The cabin door had been pushed shut and, for a brief instant, it stabilized.

Then the stern began to pull downward again.

It was the weight of the cage, Lauren realized. It was going to pull them to the bottom.

Water was pouring in through the storm-proofed portal windows. Lauren pulled at the cabin door only to find the water pressure holding it shut.

The water surface was already at her neck and, just briefly through the window, she could see the face of Captain Mundus looking through the window.

Her air-pocket was draining quickly. She had unlatched her air-tank, but she still wore it on her back. As the water rose up past her head, she snapped her clasps back on, and pulled her mask over her eyes.

She blew bubbles out of her mouthpiece even as the boat slipped beneath the surface and began to descend.

It was a slow-motion free-fall. Lauren pushed at the door, helpless against the weight of the entire boat, before turning to one of the windows, trying to wriggle her way through – absolutely impossible, even without the tank on her back.

She peered through the window and she could see the cable attached to the cage pulling them straight down.

Then there was a dull clang that seemed to ring like a physical pulse through the water. The cage had hit bottom.

A moment later, the boat itself struck the rocky ocean floor. Lauren herself was thrown roughly in that bizarrely slow-motion fashion.

The impact kicked up sand and for a long, terrifying instant, the underwater storm blocked the light, leaving her momentarily blind, before the moving tide washed the water clean.

Lauren took a moment to inventory herself – no cuts, no broken bones. She steadied her breathing before moving again to the window.

The boat had landed upside down, and as she looked outside, she realized they had landed right at the edge of the shelf – still in the relative shallows – perhaps sixty or seventy feet.

Beyond the shelf, was the drop off into the depths.

And right near the precipice, still attached by cable to the boat, was the shark cage.

The cage had landed right-side up and Lauren could see David Templeton, still locked within. He was crumpled into a ball at the foot of the cage, as if trying to hide.

Above them, the water was clear enough to see the surface, and she could see three pairs of kicking legs – so far unmolested, as the cruising shadows had once again, for the moment, disappeared.

Hiding only as far as the blue light required.

Lauren tried the door again, only to find it was now pressed against the ocean floor. She again tried the window, finding it just as small as it had been before.

For a moment, she sat still, taking advantage of the underwater dream-state to contemplate her situation.

In her vest-pocket was her phone – water-proof – up to this point a novelty underwater.

She tapped the screen alive, the blue light illuminating the dark cabin.

Lauren thought a moment, wondering how best to save her life.

Then she touched a number and began to text.

CHAPTER 18

As it turned out, Cody had actually been waiting on the call. Not THIS call, of course, but he'd been edgy all day. He knew Lauren was going out on David Templeton's charter this morning, and if he hadn't heard from her by early evening, he'd resolved to call her himself.

Ostensibly, it was about his agreement to not go public before she did – which she seemed to be honoring – albeit in sort of a nasty, Monkey's Paw, screw-you, kind of way – and he wanted to follow through on his own end.

On the other hand, he found that he didn't like Templeton hanging around her.

He had no specifically logical reason for it – sure, he hated the guy in what he acknowledged was the simple childish way of holding a grudge for a tattletale – and it was hardly like Lauren wasn't already on the guy's side of the fence anyway. He basically hated her too, after all. In moments where he hadn't blamed himself for the split, he'd blamed Lauren.

She just... looked so damn much like her. And in so many obvious ways, *was* like her.

Except where she wasn't. Cody suspected he would never have had to apply his own brakes to slow Lauren down. In fact, in Cody's absence, he was willing to bet Lauren *had* been the brakes.

Short version, she was him. That's why they hated each other.

But now, with her hanging around David Templeton – was he actually jealous?

Cody lay back on his couch and shut his eyes, controlling his breath, as if on a dive, deliberately, physically calming his nerves.

It worked sometimes. It wasn't like he'd been on an emotional roller coaster for the last few days. He felt the fading suck-mark on his neck. It wasn't like EVERYONE had.

Perhaps out of sheer stubbornness, Cody was determined to be the adult in the room, at least until this brief little stage-play of his life was over. When he talked to Lauren tonight, he would satisfy himself that the dangers south of Surf Shore would be made public, and thereby his responsibly would be ended – to Carson, to Lauren, and to the general public.

All-around good-guy, going forward, and then he would make his exit from these people's lives forever.

Lauren's text however, had sent him running out the front door in a sprint.

His small apartment was only a few blocks from the docks where he parked his boat, but he still spun the wheels off his truck as he slid into the road.

As he peeled through the streets, slipping past cars and pedestrians, leaving shaking fists behind him, he pulled out his phone and dialed the Coast Guard emergency line.

The professional female voice picked up. "Coast Guard, what's your emergency?"

Cody leaned on the clutch, revving the back-firing engine down the last straightaway to the beach.

"I need Lieutenant Quinton Shaw," Cody shouted over the engine. "Right away! Personal emergency!"

There was a brief pause, and Cody could hear the dispatcher debating making an issue of it but, perhaps hearing the tone of his voice, said, "One minute, sir, I'm switching you over."

Hold-messaging came on, offering alternate numbers and websites.

Cody knew Lieutenant Shaw had never much liked him – he'd always played at the big-brother thing with Carson, and he had looked at Cody as a bit of a bad element.

Ahead, the dock was coming up fast, and Cody hit the brakes, sliding up clear through the parking spot, over the curb, into the landscaping overlooking the dock, before skidding to a stop, wheels dug deep into the grass. With his phone still to his ear, waiting on hold, he leaped out, running full-tilt for the docks.

"Hey!" a voice shouted. "What the hell?" The dock foreman was walking up angrily to meet him, pointing at his abandoned truck - but Cody pushed past him on the run, knocking him off his feet, as he pounded down the dock, leaping bodily into his little boat.

The foreman was back on his feet, cursing. "I'm calling the cops, asshole!"

"You do that!" Cody hollered back, as he tossed his mooring and gunned the engine alive, turning with the wake out into the bay.

At his ear, there was now the steady beep of a line on hold.

Cody gunned the throttle, steering south for Surf Shore.

CHAPTER 19

The peninsula lay just ahead. Cody checked his watch – he'd been on the water nearly twenty-minutes – how much time did that leave her?

Lieutenant Shaw had been more receptive than Cody had expected when he'd finally picked up the line. He'd known Carson and Lauren for a long time. As it happened, the Guard's emergency line had already received several text messages from Lauren herself – each one identifying Cody as able to pinpoint her location, and supplying his number. Shaw had not yet personally received the message, but the rescue team was already prepping both the chopper and boats. And even as he spoke, Cody heard several messages beeping on his line – the Coast Guard operator trying to find him.

"I'll coordinate back here," Shaw had told him. "You just get out there and find her. We'll meet you there."

Cody activated the GPS tracker on his dash. "I'm already on the water," he said. "Follow my signal."

How many minutes ago had that been? He glanced nervously over his shoulder. No chopper yet.

Cody steered into deep water, pulling full throttle. On the good side, the ocean was calm today – he could see off in the distance over relatively flat swells.

On the distant horizon, he could see whale spouts, although they were too far away to tell what they were. Humpbacks? Grays?

Maybe orcas?

You know, Cody thought, that couldn't hurt.

He tapped the CD player on his dash and cranked the volume to full blast.

Echoing orca cries broadcast out into the surrounding water.

As a deterrent, this was one he hadn't seen definitively proven – although he believed the principle was sound.

On the other hand, he also still had several canisters of liquefied shark guts.

And also...

Beneath the canisters of chemical repellent, was one little toy he hadn't shown to Lauren. In a sealed case was a half-meter metal bar, looking rather like the detached barrel of a shotgun – which was basically exactly what it was – an underwater gun, called a 'powerhead', designed specifically to kill sharks underwater.

The drawback, of course, was that it had to be pressed against the shark's head. That close with a shark like, oh say, Big Rhonda, and you were already half-passed screwed.

As the peninsula drew near, Cody pulled out his phone and tapped Lauren's number.

"I'm getting close. Can you see the surface?"

A moment later, the text came back, "Yes."

"Text me when you can see my wake."

Cody glanced over his shoulder again. Where was the damned chopper? It should at least be in the air by now. He checked his watch again. Minutes were going to count here.

He crested the peninsula and began to veer in towards shore. Ahead, the dark blue of the depths was broken where the coast shelf broke away.

And in the water just beyond the shelf was a floating mass.

It was smaller than the whale they'd found the other day. But the true import didn't strike him until he was close enough to see what it was.

A baby orca.

With BIG bites taken out of it.

A cold vulnerable feeling washed through him, like ice water injected into the bloodstream.

If something down there was hitting orcas...

Cody did a quick appraisal of his suddenly fragile-looking boat.

He thought of the spouts he'd seen off in the distance – if that had actually been another orca pod, was it possible there was a shark that was actually *driving* them off?

"We might be in trouble, here," he said aloud, glancing uncomfortably at the surrounding water.

At that moment, a text-message beeped on his phone.

Lauren: "I can see you. Rhonda's circling below."

Having no idea what he was going to do, Cody grabbed up his mask and air-tank, and began to strap it on.

CHAPTER 20

Lauren had been watching the gauge on her air-tank as it ticked off minute by minute.

Less than twenty yards away, David Templeton was now standing in the cage. He likely had no idea Lauren was down here with him. Lauren estimated he had already been down for over twenty-minutes off of a roughly sixty-minute tank before the boat had gone down – and that was assuming calm breathing – likely not the case.

Lauren had sent messages to every emergency number she could think of.

She had received several messages back – Coast Guard dispatchers, mostly promising response, asking specifics.

Concentrating on tapping keys, as calmly as sitting at a desk, helped her control her breathing. She had an hour-long tank too – more if she could make it last. And according to multiple messages – the last from Lieutenant Shaw – rescue was coming.

The first response to her texts, however, had been from Cody, less than thirty seconds after she'd sent it. "I'm on my way."

While they waited, she and David Templeton together watched those left swimming on the surface get taken. One at a time.

None of them had been out-and-out Polaris attacks – just simple little sidle-up and chomp, feeding-style bites.

The big shadows above her seemed to cruise in patterns. Big Rhonda had drifted out of sight again – perhaps part of the bite-and-retreat hunting tactic, ingrained over millions of years – and the others had started filtering back in.

The first of them – she couldn't tell who from the bottom, but it was a big male – perhaps Mack the Knife – had cruised easily to where the three men had gathered together in a survivor's circle. The big male had grabbed one of them – again, Lauren couldn't tell who – by the leg. And while the clouding blood made it difficult to see, it appeared the leg was taken off near the hip. The body was dragged a few feet below the surface before falling away, the shark retreating with the meaty limb.

On the surface, one of the pairs of kicking legs made as if to follow the shark, perhaps with the intent of aiding his fellow. The other pair of legs began to kick in the direction of shore.

Both were taken in quick succession – several sharks this time, all attracted by the cloud of blood.

Somebody's missing arm drifted down past Lauren's window, missing the edge of the shelf and tumbling down into the abyss.

In his cage, Templeton had seen it too. That was when he stood and began working at the top hatchway to the cage.

Lauren looked at her own gauge, wondering how long he had left.

But if either of them swam for the surface – even if they made it – they would be sitting ducks with a mile swim towards shore.

Besides that, Lauren was still, so far, quite trapped in the cabin. She continued working at the window. The door was forced shut with the weight of the entire boat lying upon it. The window was likewise too small. However, the space cut out of the cabin wall to fit the glass was theoretically large enough to slip through if she could just get the metal frame removed – but for that she needed tools.

She had, of course, found the onboard toolbox. It was bolted to the deck just outside the door she couldn't open.

But even if she could make it out, what then? She couldn't go to the surface. And then there was that mile to a sheer cliff wall.

Lauren wondered if she could possibly make it from the bottom – just hiding, and tucking down near the rocks, and making her way to shore.

But with every minute that passed, that option – sketchy as it was – became less viable. It would take her forever to make shore, let alone a spot that wasn't sheer rock – the seal colony was still all the way around the peninsula.

Then she would be a moving target for any rescuers that might be coming her way – and she knew for a fact that they were.

Part of it was the urge to be proactive, combined with the urge to flee.

She had, however, while rummaging through the up-ended cabin, found a small back-up air-tank – the sort that divers often wore as a spare – perhaps twenty-minutes' worth. She tested it, briefly.

Twenty-minutes. It might make a difference.

Of course, there was still David Templeton.

Lauren saw he had managed to open the hatch, but yet remained inside, his head poking furtively out the top.

That meant he wasn't out yet, but he was getting close.

Lauren tapped up her phone screen again, finding the number he had given her, typing out a quick message.

Across the way, Templeton suddenly started, his hands suddenly slapping to his pockets. Lauren could see him discovering his phone, and reading his message.

After a moment, a message came back.

"I'm almost out of air."

Lauren typed back. "I've called for help. How long have you got?"

From Templeton: "My last bar's gone."

Lauren glanced at the spare tank – the one she had been counting on herself.

She eyed the open shelf between her and the cage. He could make it over here if he stayed low.

But she found herself shamefully reluctant to tell him. It wasn't like they were exactly friends. It was her own life, after all, that was at stake here.

She saw him start to climb out of the cage.

Lauren couldn't let him do it. Besides, if he could make it to the boat, he might be able to help her get out of here. She sent out the text.

Templeton, however, did not respond. He was sitting crouched atop his cage, and now he was holding his speargun – chosen because it had looked so big and impressive in the store. It would probably just piss-off any of the sharks circling above. Let alone Rhonda.

Or Mary, Lauren thought dismally – hadn't seen her in a minute, remember. That meant she was just waiting to come up from behind.

Lauren sent a second text, but Templeton was ignoring it – just like those pesky danger signals that rose the hair on your neck.

Evolved human.

Templeton pushed off the cage, swimming deliberately slowly for the surface – text-book scuba-diving instruction – the sort you got on day one.

Lauren tried one more text. This one actually seemed to get his attention as his hand reached for the pocket.

That was, however, the moment when two large sharks – two big males, this time – circled in out of the half-light over the abyss.

Templeton had raised his speargun, trying to point at both of them at once. When the first one circled too close, he poked at it aggressively, and it veered off, seemingly unperturbed. The other one, however, took the opportunity to move in from below.

Lauren had heard about Polaris attacks underwater. It tended to happen in very clear water where the sweet-spot of invisibility matched with their camouflage at a somewhat deeper level than the choppy coast.

Or, Lauren thought, when the target was just there.

It took him dead center in a single strike. The other shark turned back quickly, as if with a coordinated effort and the two of them tore David Templeton apart.

The cloud of blood was bigger than before, hiding some of the specifics. The currents, however, cleansed the water clean soon enough for Lauren to see both big animals disappearing into the surrounding mist.

She checked her air-gauge. Her heartbeat had gone up significantly, and she deliberately forced her breathing to slow.

Drifting down from above, came David Templeton's speargun. It had never even been fired. It settled with a tiny puff of sea-dust as it landed on the shelf floor.

She hiccupped a breath of despair – an involuntary sob – before she choked herself up again. Her air-gauge was well into its last bar. She would have to switch to the spare tank soon.

She shut her eyes to wait.

Then in the ponderous echo of the ocean, she heard the drone of a boat motor.

In her hand, her phone started buzzing.

CHAPTER 21

Diving into that water was maybe the hardest thing Cody had ever done.

What prompted the impulse, he wondered? What forced him over the side for a virtual stranger? And yet it seemed the almost involuntary action of throwing one's self in front of a bullet for a loved one.

Carson at second hand? Was it that simple?

He supposed it didn't really matter in the end. Whatever it was, it was enough to get him moving. He didn't kid himself there was almost anyone else in the world he would have dived down there for.

Seventy feet, straight down. That's all it was. Less than a ten-minute dive, there and back.

That's how you had to think of it – by the mechanics. Establish the risk, and work within the perimeters.

All he needed was to figure out what the hell he was going to do once he got there.

Before he got in, he better have a plan. First, he had to get her out of the boat.

He took stock of what he had available – his small boat had a winch – not enough to pull the floundered charter boat to the surface, but he should be able to shift it sufficiently. Of course, that left the issue of attaching the cable.

He had considered simply lowering the line down with a hook, but the currents were too strong to do that freehand from the surface. Someone below would have to hook it up. Lauren was trapped.

That meant a back and forth trip from the bottom to the surface. Basically, right through the death zone.

As he looked down into the water, it appeared deceptively empty. But he knew better. A floating carcass would be being guarded, likely from just out of sight, directly below – most likely from just off the side of the cliff.

The water was clear and he could see where the ocean broke off with the shelf. The boat was a dark mass just at the edge of the plateau.

Seventy feet, he thought. There and back.

He did what he could to summon confidence. His speakers had been blaring orca sounds from a mile away – a technique he believed had merit – but he wasn't about to stake the next ten minutes on a sonic scarecrow.

On a more reassuring note, he did still have four canisters of the same chemical repellent that had scattered the sharks in the area a week before.

Or at least he thought it did.

And it had tested well.

Of course, the currents were strong. The scent would be quickly washed away.

No reason for this to be easy, he thought.

He popped the tab on the first canister, dropping it in the water, watching it spin and twist in the water with the released pressure, spouting the noxious chemical into the surrounding water. He dropped a second one behind it.

Taking a breath, he took a deliberate moment to compose himself – the forced calm of a professional diver. A teacher. A guy who lived on the ocean.

He would follow the cans to the bottom, staying within the protective chemical cloud.

It *should* work.

In his vest pocket were the last two cans of repellent.

In one hand, he clutched a length of cable, with a weighted grappling hook to pull him down. In his other hand, he gripped the powerhead.

He was utterly terrified.

A kernel of cowardice disguised as common sense told him he wouldn't do her any good if he was killed, and that he should wait for the Coast Guard.

But as of yet, there was no chopper, and no boats. How far out were they? Ten, fifteen minutes? And then, how long to get something done?

Long enough. Too long.

Cody shut his eyes. Get away from the surface, he thought. Go straight for the bottom.

He fell over the side and kicked his way down into the gray-blue darkness.

CHAPTER 22

The boat had narrowly missed the tumble into the deeper depths. Ten more feet and it would be teetering on the edge of the underwater shelf. As Cody drew near the bottom, letting the boat hook pull him like an anchor, he also saw the empty shark cage, still attached to the winch.

That, he thought, was something he might make use of.

But first thing's first.

For the moment, the circling shapes seemed to have retreated. That, unfortunately, was both good and bad. Even more than the wolf in the woods, it was the shark you couldn't see that you had to worry about.

Cody could see why this spot had become an anchor point for Great Whites. It was perfect. Ten feet beyond the crest of the shelf, the water was deep enough that you could no longer see even a hint of the bottom. The blue just continued on up to the point where the light simply faded away.

That was the twilight where the sharks prowled – just at the moment they became invisible.

To you.

They could see you just fine.

He felt immeasurably better once his feet hit the hard, sandy surface of the shelf bottom. Using the heavy grappling hook as an anchor, he pulled himself over to the sunken boat.

Inside, Lauren was peering out the upturned window. Her hand reached out the small gap. She tapped at the final bar on her air-gauge.

Cody nodded, grabbing her hand in attempted reassurance.

Lauren turned away, reappearing at the window, holding a small reserve tank.

A moment later, Cody's pocket buzzed.

The text message on his phone read. "I've got twenty-minutes."

Cody glanced cautiously over his shoulder. The currents here were strong, right at the edge of the crest – like wind gusts through a canyon.

The residue of the chemical repellent would be washed away quickly. He had two cans left. He'd planned on using at least one to swim back through on the way to the surface. Two would have been better. But that still left the problem of getting Lauren herself back to the surface, once he'd gotten the boat off of her.

In the optimistic hope that it could be so easy, Cody gave an experimental pull on the over-turned railing. If he could simply shift the boat a few feet off the floor, that might provide enough room for Lauren to wriggle out the cabin door.

The entire weight of the boat, however, was against him. He couldn't even rock it, not even with the aid of the water.

He sighed bubbles – that would have been too easy.

His phone beeped again.

"The toolbox," it said. "Take out the window frame."

Cody looked under the deck, through the narrow space between the rocks, where the closed chest was bolted from the upside-down floorboards.

It was dark under the boat. Using his phone light, he felt along the sealed chest, before finding it locked.

Cody's blood-pressure kicked up a notch in frustration. He took a deliberate breath, dealing with each issue as it came.

The key was likely in the cabin. Hopefully in a drawer. He started to text Lauren to look for it, but then his eyes found something else strapped under the railing, next to the life-jackets.

A large yellow package, two-feet by two-feet – flat like a folded towel.

Cody snatched it up and slipped out from beneath the wrecked boat.

As he did so, his phone buzzed in his hands, the message blinking.

"They're back. Be careful."

Cody poked his head out cautiously, like an angelfish out of an anemone. He saw nothing immediately, but as he focused on the outer dimness, he thought he saw a circling shadow.

He pulled out one of the last two canisters and pulled the tab.

Holding the can as it sprayed into the current, Cody held the cloud close to him and the ocean floor, out of the current as best he could.

When he was satisfied the dim shadows had retreated, he pulled himself out from under the wreck and swam up to Lauren's window.

She had jettisoned her big tank and had replaced it with the back-up – a simple mouthpiece with a miniature tank on the end of it.

Her eyes were wide behind her mask.

It was her eyes, Cody thought, where she looked like Carson the most.

He held up the package he'd pulled from beneath the deck, showing her the label that said 'inflatable life-raft'. He typed a quick message.

"I'm going to get you out of there."

He positioned the raft between the over-turned stern and the rocky bottom, taking a moment to find the best leverage point possible, all the while conscious of what might be lurking just over his shoulder.

Pushing back out from under the boat, he pulled the cord.

There was an explosion of angry bubbles and there was the sensation of being hit bodily with a large feather pillow – enough to knock him over backwards.

The boat lurched as the life-raft ballooned to full-size. The space between the deck and the floor rose nearly a foot-and-a-half.

Cody darted back under the boat, warily conscious of the weight above him as it creaked and rocked with the flow of the current, and he pulled at the cabin door, even as Lauren herself started to push her way out from inside.

The door, unfortunately, was only able to open barely a foot –
and with the awkward angle, Lauren still found herself trapped as
thoroughly as before.

As the boat swayed and creaked above them, their eyes met
through their masks, and Cody thought he saw the first hint of
despair. He grabbed her hand through the space in the door. Then
he pointed to his phone, typing out a message.

"I've still got the cable. I'm going to hook it up, and swim for
the surface. I can winch the boat off of you."

He pointed to where the cage sat a short distance away.

"Once you're out, you attach the cable to the cage, and I'll pull
you up."

Lauren squeezed his hand. Behind her mask, she shut her
eyes. But she nodded.

Slipping back out into open water, Cody pulled the cable to
the back of the boat to the gaping hole where the motor had
apparently been torn loose.

Bitten loose, he corrected himself, unhappily.

There was still a solid cleat left at a structural girder point on
the railing, and he attached the hook.

Then he glanced up to the surface – attractive and inviting, his
boat rolling serenely with the waves. So close – not even a sixty
second swim.

Yet still so far.

He looked down at the remaining canister in his hand.

Use it?

Or perhaps leave it down here with Lauren, for when she had
to make her way to the cage? He raised his other hand where he
still held the powerhead – puny looking as it might be.

What to do?

Not yet, he decided, tucking the canister into his vest pocket.
He would keep it with him – handy if he needed it on the way up –
and once the boat was off her, he would drop it back down as she
made her way to the cage.

Perfect plan.

Lauren was tapping the window, pointing at her air-tank.

Cody nodded. He typed in a message.

"I'm going up now."

She nodded back.

Cody glanced around at the misty blue water as he pushed himself off the bottom, following his cable on the way up, thinking of the abalone divers as he went – hit from below when they surfaced – torn apart – never saw it coming.

And the moment he moved, was when Rhonda attacked.

CHAPTER 23

Great White Sharks are known to attack either vertically or horizontally. While the vast majority of attacks on humans occur at the surface, there were a significant proportion of FATAL attacks that happened underwater.

There were a number of good reasons for this, the first, and most obvious being, that a diver hit underwater, besides being bitten, also had the added threat of drowning.

Then there was the environment where such linear attacks were likely to occur – almost exclusively in high-current areas – such as where abalone hunters dive. In the fast currents, sharks targeted seals feeding on the abalone, and a man in a wetsuit, under such conditions, would trigger a similar, sideways Polaris response.

Such rip-currents existed right where they were now. It was almost text-book.

Rhonda charged out of the gloom as if she'd been waiting for him – and likely she had been. The speed with which she moved brought up images of stepping in front of a speeding car – looking up in time enough to see it – not near time enough to get out of the way.

Cody hadn't even had time to get the powerhead in front of him when Big Rhonda struck.

He HAD, however, been pulling himself up along the cable to the surface, and as such, there was a line of stiff steel wire between him and the oncoming jaws.

It was the shark's own reflex that saved him. When the snout touched the cable, it activated a response Cody had actually seen researchers demonstrate in the wild. A hand touching the tip of the nose short-circuited a shark's senses, and would induce a brief moment of tonic-immobility, causing the shark to stiffen up, its mouth to gape, and leaving it in a few seconds of paralysis.

Cody had been attempting to twist out of the way, but Rhonda's sudden jerk to the side turned the teeth away from him, and he was instead struck with a physical blow of simple impact.

Which, Cody thought, as the unbelievable weight struck him, was still like getting hit by a moving car. Or in this case, a submarine.

He was knocked backwards, his breath cruelly driven from his lungs, with his mask and mouthpiece flying off over his head. His tank blowing precious oxygen into the surrounding water, he had just enough time to see Lauren, her face pressed to the window, screaming bubbles, before he was dragged over the top and out of her sight.

Cody grasped blindly for his mouthpiece, pulling his mask back on, fighting to see through the furious bubbles.

The bubbles themselves seemed to further confuse the momentarily disoriented shark, and its head jerked back and forth, as if trying to recover its target.

Cody had been knocked back into the hull of the boat, and when he looked up, he saw the water around him bloody. The impact had left cuts. The spot where Rhonda had struck, glancing blow or not, might have left a broken rib or two.

In any case, it hurt to breathe.

Not five feet away, Rhonda was nosing forward, rooting him out as he ducked between the sunken hull and the rocks behind. The big shark's head jerked back and forth, recovering her senses after the physiological equivalent of an electric shock. She veered towards him again.

Cody reached for the remaining canister in his pocket, and found it gone.

Rhonda struck the boat's hull, knocking it against the rocks – not a full-on charge, but a show of power.

Territorial attacks, Cody remembered, were even worse than predatory ones, Cody remembered. That was when they were in a fight – when they kept coming back.

This was a shark that had hit an orca, after all. And in fact, as he thought about it, that might be why the orca cries, which he could hear even now, echoing like elevator music through the water, hadn't scared her off.

Could it be that, after having been run out of the Farallons, this particular big fish had decided to take a stand – socio-biological evolution at play? Big Rhonda was gunning for top predator of the ocean – and was apparently territorial enough to challenge even orcas.

Or, for that matter, any boat that happened along.

As he crouched among the rocks, Cody's finger slid over the trigger of the powerhead.

Because now he knew, *this* was the shark that had killed Carson. This was the one who had sunk her boat.

He found himself smiling ironically, because he knew Carson herself would have argued the point – circumstantial evidence, she would have said.

He would have rejoined willingly enough.

Circumstantial evidence, he would say, was usually the most damning. There were, after all, only a few suspects. Rhonda was the right size, right temperament, right area. Three strikes, your Honor.

But none of that mattered right now to Cody.

He knew it because he knew it. He knew it in his bones.

He was smiling now, because this was the fight he wanted.

As Rhonda made another pass just a few feet above, Cody leaped out, pressing the barrel of the powerhead against the massive head, just behind the eye, and depressed the trigger.

There was an explosion in his face, followed by a massive push of water, as Rhonda's two-and-a-half-ton body thrashed, raining down massive blows on the upturned hull and surrounding rocks. The boat itself shifted once again, as the giant fish torqued and twisted back out into open ocean. A trail of blood leaked like a facet from a softball-sized hole in her head.

Once back into open water, the big shark twitched spasmodically, before falling limp, its swimming stroke fading into a lifeless drift with the current, descending back over the shelf.

Cody watched a moment as the massive form began to slowly sink.

There was a temptation to sit and watch – a certain satisfaction to be had – revenge being a dish best served cold.

But, he thought, allowing himself nothing, there were still more sharks. And he was under time pressure.

In his pocket, his phone was buzzing. Lauren.

Cody popped his head back over the hull, looking down into her window.

Seeing him, Lauren reached through the small space to clutch his hands. Behind her mask, she was crying.

Cody gave her a reassuring squeeze, pointing at the surface.

In the cabin, Lauren nodded, tapping her wrist to indicate time.

With one last knock on her window, Cody pushed off the bottom once again, pulling himself along the cable for the boat waiting above.

And in the misty blue, beyond the shelf, Big Rhonda's floating body suddenly twitched, like a machine trying to start despite blown circuits.

Then, in the manner of someone sleeping, snapping suddenly awake, she righted herself in the water, and once again began to swim.

Above her, Cody was halfway to the surface – rising deliberately with his slowest bubble.

In leisurely fashion, Rhonda circled up from below.

CHAPTER 24

Lauren was on the last minutes of her spare air-tank. The little vessel was going dry well short of its twenty-minutes – perhaps because of her breathing, or maybe it was just low to start - perhaps old. When Cody had pushed off for the surface, she had known it was going to be close.

But when she saw Rhonda shaking off the effects of the powerhead blast to her temple, Lauren realized it was going to be a lot less than close.

In that moment, she understood that without some drastic action, she was going to die here today.

The boat had been rocked and shifted by impact, but the door to the cabin still only left a barely twelve-inch gap and, while it was still propped by the inflated life-raft, that narrow margin was now maintained the entire six or seven feet she would need to crawl out from under the upturned deck – all the while, the full weight of the boat continued to shift dramatically with each gust of the currents.

If she got stuck, she would quickly be crushed – probably simultaneously drowned.

Of course, even if she made it out, that left the even greater likelihood of being eaten.

She wondered if the Coast Guard would find her – or if whatever remained would stay down here, somewhere, alone in the dark.

Just like whatever was left of Carson.

Lauren pushed open the door, and began to wrestle her way through.

The angle of the rock allowed no freedom of movement, while above her, the boat groaned, waiting for the current to catch sufficiently for the next big shift.

She worked her head through the opening, breathing steadily, as she angled her mask and the little spare tank through the narrow gap. Then she began to wrestle her shoulders.

Her back to the sea floor, she felt suddenly light-headed. The tank was going dry.

Above her, the boat rocked ever-so-slightly, its groan turning just a touch more shrill.

Working her hips under the door, she found her legs couldn't bend correctly while lying on her back. For a moment of sheer panic, she realized she was stuck. But just before she began to thrash, she caught herself – forcing her breathing to slow, shutting her eyes.

Then, she twisted face down, grinding her face and chest into the rocks, bending her knees around the door and out.

There was a heartbeat where she allowed herself one more breath, before she scrambled out from beneath the overturned hull like a crab.

She was free.

She was also seventy-feet down with maybe one breath of air left in her tank.

And circling above, was Rhonda.

The big shark was still moving slowly – still damaged by that head blast.

Cody still didn't see her circling below – he was nearing the surface.

That would be when Rhonda would strike, Lauren thought. Just like a trigger.

She sat helpless on the bottom, looking up. As if the boat would be a safe haven, even if Cody reached it. The rules in this ecology had changed.

Which, as far as Lauren was concerned, meant other rules had too.

Lying in the sand-blasted rocky floor of the shelf, was David Templeton's speargun – the one she had frowned at – and then had scoffed over.

That didn't change the nasty barbed tip. Lauren scooted along the bottom and grabbed up the gun.

At that very moment, the air in her tank gave out.

Lauren took her last breath and began to kick slowly to the surface.

Smoothly as possible, exhaling slowly so as not to blow your lungs out.

Rhonda circled above. Cody had reached the surface.

Below him, Lauren could see Rhonda's pectoral fins flare, her back arch, pinpointing her target, invisible from above.

But just as Rhonda was invisible to Cody, so was Lauren invisible to her.

The great white target was wide and open.

As she rushed up from below to kill this animal she had worked so hard to protect all her life, Lauren felt an odd-sort of revisionist life flashing before her eyes.

It was kind of a last-minute rationalization – activated out of pure instinct for survival.

This rational turn of mind was perfectly willing to acknowledge that this was a problem animal – that area of common ground Cody had always insisted *should* have existed between them.

In a way, as she closed in on Rhonda's unsuspecting belly, she thought it was very much like being a direct part of nature. She thought Carson would have approved. She knew Cody would.

Perhaps too often, those that extolled Darwinism, somehow didn't think it actually applied to them.

Time to atone for past sins.

Lauren aimed the speargun with the sort of precision she had used with a scalpel the first time she had dissected a white shark. She fired the spear directly between its gills, aiming medically for her heart.

There was the twang of release and the spear fired home.

Lauren never knew what hit her.

Rhonda convulsed violently, twisting like a catfish, and Lauren had only a sense of movement and a flash view of the tail as she was struck bodily.

There was a sense of impact, tearing her mask away, sending her reeling, all in that same dreamlike slow-motion, and there was a second's awareness as she knew she was being knocked unconscious.

She felt her last breath go out in a stream of bubbles and the world went black.

She felt herself floating – ready to die – even accepting it.

Then there were hands on her shoulders and a mouthpiece forced between her lips.

Not fully conscious, she reflexively sucked air.

Cody held her upright in the water, still thirty feet down.

Lauren blinked awake, her vision blurry without her mask. But Cody was pointing up.

Peering into the blur, Lauren could see the mass that was Big Rhonda, floating, again, seemingly lifelessly, as she had before, the tip of the spear protruding from her vitals.

Yet, just as she had before, she began to flutter and twitch back to life again.

Cody was pulling them both to the surface, grabbing a quick breath of air for himself.

Rhonda circled in their direction.

It wasn't even going to be close.

Without her mask, the onrushing shape was nothing but a blur. Lauren shut her eyes anyway.

But as she did so, there was a sudden flash of an even bigger blur.

A rush of water sent them both tumbling, tearing them from each other's grasp, yanking the mouthpiece from Lauren's mouth.

Still twenty feet down, she swallowed water and began to choke.

Kicking madly, she bolted for the surface.

Her head broke the water, coughing and gagging, vomiting salt-water, only to have her head struck by something hard – the hull of Cody's boat – nearly knocking her unconscious once again. She swooned in the water, before she felt Cody's hands on her again, pulling her up, pulling them both to the boat, grabbing the railing and hauling them both on-board.

They collapsed together to the floor.

For several moments, they both simply lay there on the deck, gasping.

Then, right beside the boat, there was a sudden geyser-like spray of air.

A spout.

They both sat up, looking over the railing, where several towering black fins, some over six feet tall, surrounded their little boat like a grove of trees.

Orcas. Killer Whales.

And one of them, slightly smaller, with a shorter, hooked fin, cruised the surface with what remained of Big Rhonda.

The big shark had been torn apart – apparently several whales converging at once, evidently not content to simply wait and drown her with tonic immobility.

Several yards away, the dead baby orca still floated.

Lauren looked down at the whale parading its catch.

Clearly this was mama.

And it clearly answered the question as to where she had gone after her calf had been killed. She'd gone to get some friends.

Realizing his stereo was still playing full blast into the water, Cody switched off the speakers.

The orcas spent another minute or two circling their boat.

Then, as a group, they sounded, and were gone.

Lauren and Cody sat for several long moments, not speaking.

"Wow," Cody said finally. "Did that really just happen?"

Off in the distance, they heard the first drone of the Coast Guard chopper's approach.

Cody smiled. "Right on time."

He turned to Lauren, gingerly inspecting the cuts the rocks had left on her arms and face.

"Are you hurt?"

Lauren did a quick self-inspection.

"I actually think I'm okay," she said. "I can't believe it."

The Coast Guard chopper had spotted them and was circling above. Cody waved.

In his pocket, his phone rang – Lieutenant Shaw. Cody picked up and explained in a few quick sentences.

"We got her out," he said. "I'm taking her in."

"Any other survivors?" Shaw responded.

"No," Cody said, glancing to Lauren, who shook her head. "No other survivors."

"We'll need a statement from you both," Shaw said.

"See you on shore." Cody clicked off his phone, tucking it back in his pocket.

Lauren put a hand on his shoulder, pulling him around so she could look him seriously in the eye.

"Thank you," she said, "for saving my life."

Cody smiled. "I think you probably saved mine as well."

Standing there in his boat, looking up at him, Lauren thought they were going to have a moment.

Naturally, Cody rescued her from that as well.

"Although," he said thoughtfully, "it WAS you that was stuck out here in the first place. So, I guess what I did was a little more pro-active." He shrugged modestly. "Just saying."

Cody considered.

"Tell you what," he said, "just admit I was right about literally everything, and we'll call it even."

Lauren stared at him with a slow burn. "Really? Now? Have you ever heard not to kick a person when they're down?"

"I've heard that one, yes," Cody allowed.

"How about not saying, 'I told you so'?"

"Yep, heard that one too."

Lauren shook her head in amazement. "So basically, this is all my fault?"

Cody's grin broadened, and Lauren realized the set-up line too late.

"Well," he said, clearly enjoying every syllable, "you can't blame the sharks."

Cody's smile was unbearably smug as he started the boat and shifted into gear.

"What say we get you home?" he said. "The Coast Guard can clean up here."

And apparently just because he couldn't resist, he added, "Or we can stop off for a drink, if you like."

"You know," Lauren said, as they started to move, "I don't like you very much." She eyed him coldly. "At *all*."

Cody's laughter sounded over his motor as he turned them back for shore.

CHAPTER 25

The great fish hovered at the twilight between light and dark – the very moment she became invisible.

Bloody Mary was hunting.

In the way that she understood things, she realized that Big Rhonda was gone – both as a rival and a useful tool. Mary had, after all, always been the first on the scene to freeload – as she had been, in fact, not too far from here, when Rhonda had sunk Carson Sheridan's boat.

And while Rhonda had been quite interested in Carson's splashing after she had been dumped into the water after the boat had sunk, it had been the opportunistic Mary who had actually moved in quickly to snatch her, as she clung to the wreckage.

Mary had already made associations, you see.

In her own simple way, she remembered the free swim with the strange creature clinging to her dorsal fin. At the time, she had identified it for what it was – a prey item out of reach. And in the manner of her kind, she had ignored it.

Ignored it, that is, until it was no longer out of reach.

There had been no need to bump-test this time – she knew what it was – and she had simply risen up and taken Carson in a single strike.

Just as she had taken a number of surfers over the last several years.

On the other hand, Mary had also gotten a bit lazy.

Rhonda was gone. Now Mary was hungry.

The opportunistic scavenger had now been replaced by the active hunter.

And right now, about two-hundred yards from her current position, the Coast Guard was salvaging Captain Mundus' sunken boat. Several divers had been dispatched to the underwater shelf below.

Although she didn't understand the words, the sounds of radio communication traveled to Mary's sensitive ears as she cruised the perimeter, just out of sight.

Lieutenant Quinton Shaw was leading the operation. His voice cautioned his fellow divers to keep an eye out for sharks.

Someone had replied back that the appearance of the orca pod would probably be enough to keep them off.

"Probably," Shaw had answered, with emphasis.

There had been dutiful, nervous laughter.

In point of fact, Mary WAS aware of the orca pod, still lurking off the coast, and yes, it HAD scared off most of her fellows.

On the other hand, that's what the deep depths beyond the shelf were for.

As she circled closer, she could now see the divers gathered around the wreck.

In continuing passes, always out of sight, she edged ever-nearer.

Bloody Mary.

Who always appears from behind.

THE END

CHECK OUT OTHER GREAT DEEP SEA THRILLERS

THE BREACH
by **Edward J. McFadden III**

A Category 4 hurricane punched a quarter mile hole in Fire Island, exposing the Great South Bay to the ferocity of the Atlantic Ocean, and the current pulled something terrible through the new breach. A monstrosity of the past mixed with the present has been disturbed and it's found its way into the sheltered waters of Long Island's southern sea.

Nate Tanner lives in Stones Throw, Long Island. A disgraced SCPD detective lieutenant put out to pasture in the marine division because of his Navy background and experience with aquatic crime scenes, Tanner is assigned to hunt the creeper in the bay. But he and his team soon discover they're the ones being hunted.

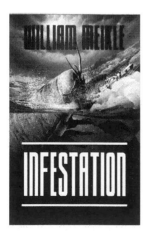

INFESTATION
by **William Meikle**

It was supposed to be a simple mission. A suspected Russian spy boat is in trouble in Canadian waters. Investigate and report are the orders.

But when Captain John Banks and his squad arrive, it is to find an empty vessel, and a scene of bloody mayhem.

Soon they are in a fight for their lives, for there are things in the icy seas off Baffin Island, scuttling, hungry things with a taste for human flesh.

They are swarming. And they are growing.

"Scotland's best Horror writer" - Ginger Nuts of Horror

"The premier storyteller of our time." - Famous Monsters of Filmland

CHECK OUT OTHER GREAT DEEP SEA THRILLERS

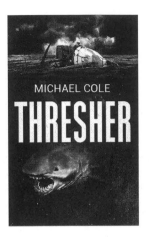

THRESHER
by **Michael Cole**

In the aftermath of a hurricane, a series of strange events plague the coastal waters off Florida. People go into the water and never return. Corpses of killer whales drift ashore, ravaged from enormous bite marks. A fishing trawler is found adrift, with a mysterious gash in its hull.

Transferred to the coastal town of Merit, police officer Leonard Riker uncovers the horrible reality of an enormous Thresher shark lurking off the coast. Forty feet in length, it has taken a territorial claim to the waters near the town harbor. Armed with three-inch teeth, a scythe-like caudal fin, and unmatched aggression, the beast seeks to kill anything sharing the waters.

THE GUILLOTINE
by **Lucas Pederson**

1,000 feet under the surface, Prehistoric Anthropologist, Ash Barrington, and his team are in the midst of a great archeological dig at the bottom of Lake Superior where they find a treasure trove of bones. Bones of dinosaurs that aren't supposed to be in this particular region. In their underwater facility, Infinity Moon, Ash and his team soon discover a series of underground tunnels. Upon exploring, they accidentally open an ice pocket, thawing the prehistoric creature trapped inside. Soon they are being attacked, the facility falling apart around them, by what Ash knows is a dunkleosteus and all those bones were from its prey. Now...Ash and his team are the prey and the creature will stop at nothing to get to them.

CHECK OUT OTHER GREAT DEEP SEA THRILLERS

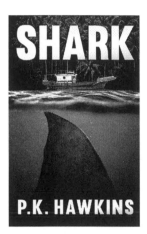

SHARK: INFESTED WATERS
by P.K. Hawkins

For Simon, the trip was supposed to be a once in a lifetime gift: a journey to the Amazon River Basin, the land that he had dreamed about visiting since he was a child. His enthusiasm for the trip may be tempered by the poor conditions of the boat and their captain leading the tour, but most of the tourists think they can look the other way on it. Except things go wrong quickly. After a horrific accident, Simon and the other tourists find themselves trapped on a tiny island in the middle of the river. It's the rainy season, and the river is rising. The island is surrounded by hungry bull sharks that won't let them swim away. And worst of all, the sharks might not be the only blood-thirsty killers among them. It was supposed to be the trip of a lifetime. Instead, they'll be lucky if they make it out with their lives at all.

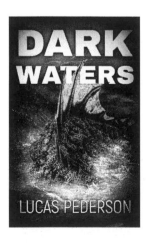

DARK WATERS
by Lucas Pederson

Jörmungandr is an ancient Norse sea monster. Thought to be purely a myth until a battleship is torn a part by one.

With his brother on that ship, former Navy Seal and deep-sea diver, Miles Raine, sets out on a personal vendetta against the creature and hopefully save his brother. Bringing with him his old Seal team, the Dagger Points, they embark on a mission that might very well be their last.

But what happens when the hunters become the hunted and the dark waters reveal more than a monster?

Made in the USA
Middletown, DE
06 July 2020